Samuel Adams Drake

The Campaign of Trenton

1776-77

Samuel Adams Drake

The Campaign of Trenton
1776-77

ISBN/EAN: 9783337425746

Printed in Europe, USA, Canada, Australia, Japan

Cover: Foto ©Andreas Hilbeck / pixelio.de

More available books at **www.hansebooks.com**

CONTENTS

(5)

PRELUDE

SELDOM, in the annals of war, has a single campaign witnessed such a remarkable series of reverses as did that which began at Boston in March, 1776, and ended at Morristown in January, 1777. Only by successive defeats did our home-made generals and our rustic soldiery learn their costly lesson that war is not a game of chance, or mere masses of men an army.

Though costly, this sort of discipline, this education, gradually led to a closer equality between the combatants, as year after year they faced and fought each other. When the lesson was well learned our generals began to win battles, and our soldiers to fight with a confidence altogether new to them. In vain do we look for any other explanation of the sudden stiffening up of the backbone of the Revolutionary army, or of the equally sudden restoration of an apparently dead and buried cause after even its most devoted followers

had given up all as lost. As with expiring breath
that little band of hunted fugitives, miserable remnant of an army of 30,000 men, turning suddenly
upon its victorious pursuers, dealt it blow after
blow, the sun which seemed setting in darkness,
again rose with new splendor upon the fortunes
of these infant States.

Certainly the military, political, and moral effects
of this brilliant finish to what had been a losing
campaign, in which almost each succeeding day
ushered in some new misfortune, were prodigious.
But neither the importance nor the urgency of this
masterly counter-stroke to the American cause
can be at all appreciated, or even properly under-
stood, unless what had gone before, what in fact
had produced a crisis so dark and threatening, is
brought fully into light. Washington himself says
the act was prompted by a dire necessity. Coming from him, these words are full of meaning.
We realize that the fate of the Revolution was
staked upon this one last throw. If we would take
the full measure of these words of his, spoken in
the fullest conviction of their being final words, we
must again go over the whole field, strewed with

dead hopes, littered with exploded reputations, cumbered with cast-off traditions, over which the patriot army marched to its supreme trial out into the broad pathway which led to final success.

The campaign of 1776 is, therefore, far too instructive to be studied merely with reference to its crowning and concluding feature. In considering it the mind is irresistibly impelled toward one central, statuesque figure, rising high above the varying fortunes of the hour, like the Statue of Liberty out of the crash and roar of the surrounding storm.

Nowhere, we think, does Washington appear to such advantage as during this truly eventful campaign. Though sometimes troubled in spirit, he is always unshaken. Though his army was a miserable wreck, driven about at the will of the enemy, Washington was ever the rallying-point for the handful of officers and men who still surrounded him. If the cause was doomed to shipwreck, we feel that he would be the last to leave the wreck.

His letters, written at this trying period, are characterized by that same even tone, as they disclose in more prosperous times. He does not dare to be hopeful, yet he will not give up beaten. There is an atmosphere of stern, though dignified determination about him, at this trying hour, which, in a man of his admirable equipoise, is a thing for an enemy to beware of. In a word, Washington driven into a corner was doubly dangerous. And it is evident that his mind, roused to unwonted activity by the gravity of the crisis, the knowledge that all eyes turned to him, sought only for the opportune moment to show forth its full powers, and by a conception of genius dominate the storm of disaster around him.

Washington never claimed to be a man of destiny. He never had any nicknames among his soldiers. Napoleon was the " Little Corporal," " Marlborough " " Corporal John," Wellington the " Iron Duke," Grant the " Old Man," but there seems to have been something about the personality of Washington that forbade any thought of familiarity, even on the part of his trusty veterans. Yet their faith in him was such that, as Wellington once said of his Peninsular army, they would have gone anywhere with him, and he could have done anything with them.

THE CAMPAIGN OF TRENTON

I

NEW YORK THE SEAT OF WAR

UPON finding that what had at first seemed only a local rebellion was spreading like wildfire throughout the length and breadth of the colonies, that bloodshed had united the people as one man, **New views** and that these people were everywhere **of the war.** getting ready for a most determined resistance, the British ministry awoke to the necessity of dealing with the revolt, in this its newer and more dangerous aspect, as a fact to be faced accordingly, and its military measures were, therefore, no longer directed to New England exclusively, but to the suppression of the rebellion as a whole. For this purpose New York was very judiciously chosen as the true base of operations.[1]

In the colonies, the news of great preparations then making in England to carry out this policy, inevitably led up to the same conclusions, but as the siege of Boston had not yet drawn to a close, very little could be done by way of making ready to meet this new and dangerous emergency.

We must now first look at the ways and means.

A new army had been enlisted in the trenches before Boston to take the place of that first one, whose term of service expired with the new year,

The new Continental Army.
1776. On paper it consisted of twenty-eight battalions, with an aggregate of 20,372 officers and men. By the actual returns, made up shortly before the army marched for New York, there were 13,145 men of all arms then enrolled, of whom not more than 9,500 were reported as fit for duty. These were all Continentals,[2] as the regular troops were then called, to distinguish them from the militia.

Immediately upon the evacuation of Boston by the British (March 17, 1776), the army marched by divisions to New York, the last brigade, with

It marches to New York.
the commander-in-chief, leaving Cambridge on April 4.[3] This move dis-

tinctly foreshadows the general opinion that the
seat of war was about to be transferred to New
York and its environs.

There is no need to discuss the general proposi-
tion, so quickly accepted by both belligerents, as
regards the strategic value of New York for com-
bined operations by land and sea. Hence the
Americans were naturally unwilling to abandon it
to the enemy. A successful defence was really
beyond their abilities, however, against such a
powerful fleet as was now coming to attack them,
because this fleet could not be prevented from
forcing its way into the upper bay without strong
fortifications at the Narrows to stop it, and these
the Americans did not have. Once in possession
of the navigable waters, the enemy could cut off
communication in every direction, as well as
choose his own point of attack. Afraid, however,
of the moral effect of giving up the city without a
struggle, the Americans were led into the fatal
error of squandering their resources upon a
defence which could end only in one way, instead
of holding the royal army besieged, as had been
so successfully done at Boston.

Having arrived at New York, Washington's force was increased by the two or three thousand men who had been hastily summoned for its defence,[4] and who were then busily employed in throwing up works at various points, under the direction of the engineers.

Now, it is usual to call such a large body of raw recruits, badly armed, and without discipline, an army, in the same breath as a well armed and thoroughly disciplined body. This one had done good service behind entrenchments, and in some minor operations at Boston had shown itself possessed of the best material, but the situation was now to be wholly reversed, the besiegers were to become the besieged, their mistakes were to be turned against them, the experiments of inexperi-**Make-up of** ence were to be tested at the risk of **the army.** total failure, and the *morale* severely tried by the grumbling and discontent arising for the most part from laxity of discipline, but somewhat so, too, from the wretched administration of the various civil departments of the army.[5] The officers did not know how to instruct their men, and the men could not be made to take proper

care of themselves. In consequence of this state
of things, inseparable perhaps from the existing
conditions, General Heath tells us that by the first
week of August the number of sick amounted to
near 10,000 men, who were to be met with lying
"in almost every barn, stable, shed, and even
under the fences and bushes," about the camps.
This primary element of disintegration is always
one of the worst possible to deal with in an army
of citizen soldiers, and the present case proved no
exception.

Except a troop of Connecticut light-horse, who
had been curtly and imprudently dismissed because
they showed sufficient *esprit de corps* to demur
against doing guard duty as infantry, and whose
absence was only too soon to be dearly atoned for,
there was no cavalry, not even for patrols, outposts, or vedettes. These being thus of necessity
drawn from the infantry, it was usual to see them
come back into camp with the enemy close at their
heels, instead of giving the alarm in season to get
the troops under arms.

As for the infantry, it was truly a motley assem-
blage. A few of the regiments, raised in the cities,

were tolerably well armed and equipped, and some
few were in uniform.   But in general they wore the
same homespun in which they had left their homes,
even to the field officers, who were only distin-
guished by their red cockades.   In few regiments
were the arms all of one kind, not a few had only
a sprinkling of   ats, while some companies,
whom it had been found impracticable to furnish
with fire arms at the home rendezvous, carried the
old-fashioned pikes of by-gone days.   Among the
good, bad, and indifferent, Washington had had
two thousand militia poured in upon him, without
any arms whatever.   But these men could use
pick and spade.

The single regiment of artillery this "rabble
army," as Knox calls it, could boast was unquestionably its most reliable arm.   Under Knox's able
direction it was getting into fairly good shape,
though the guns were of very light metal.   In the
early conflicts around New York it was rather too
lavishly used, and suffered accordingly, but its
efficiency was so marked as to draw forth the admission from a British officer of rank that the rebel
artillery officers were at least equal to their own.

These plain facts speak for themselves. If radical defects of organization lay behind them, it was not the fault of Washington or the army, but is rather attributable to the want of any settled policy or firm grasp of the situation on the part of the Congress.

Washington had no ill .. ther with regard to himself or his soldiers. His letters of this date prove this. He was as well aware ais own shortcomings as a general, as of those of his men as soldiers. There could, perhaps, be no greater proof of the solidity of his judgment than this capacity to estimate himself correctly, free from all the prickings of personal vanity or popular praise. With reference to the army he probably thought that if raw militia would fight so well behind breastworks at Bunker Hill, they could be depended upon to do so elsewhere, under the same conditions. His idea, therefore, was to fight only in intrenched positions, and this was the general plan of campaign for 1776.[6]

---

[1] As will be seen farther on, New England had no strategic value in this relation.

[2] CONTINENTALS. This term, for want of a better, arose from the

practice of speaking of the colonies, as a whole, as the Continent, to distinguish them from this or that one, separately.

³ THE last brigade to march at this time is meant. As a matter of fact one brigade was left at Boston, as a guard against accidents. Later on it joined Washington.

⁴ GENERAL LEE had been sent to New York as early as January. He took military possession of the city, with militia furnished by Connecticut.

⁵ IN a private letter General Knox indignantly styles it "this rabble army."

⁶ " BEING fully persuaded that it would be presumption to draw out our young troops into open ground against their superiors, both in numbers and discipline, I have never spared the spade and pickaxe."— *Letters.*

II

PLANS FOR DEFENCE

WASHINGTON'S army had no sooner reached the Hudson than ten of the best battalions [1] were hurried off to Albany, if possible, to retrieve the disasters which had recently overwhelmed the army of Canada, where three generals, two of whom, Montgomery and Thomas, were of the highest promise, with upwards of 5,000 men, had been lost. The departure of these seasoned troops made a gap not easily filled, and should not be lost sight of in reckoning the effectiveness of what were left.

Troops sent to Canada.

This large depletion was, however, more than made good, in numbers at least, by the reënforcements now arriving from the middle colonies, who, with troops forming the garrison of the city, presently raised the whole force under Washington's orders [2] to a much larger number than were ever assembled in one body again.

Strength of the army.

A very large proportion, however, were militia-
men, called out for a few weeks only, who indeed
served to swell the ranks, without adding much
real strength to the army.

It being fully decided upon that New York
should be held, two entirely distinct sets of measures were found indispensable. First the city was
commanded by Brooklyn Heights, rising at short

Plans for defence.   cannon-shot across the East River.
These heights were now being strongly
fortified on the water-side against the enemy's
fleet, and on the land-side against a possible attack
by his land forces.[3]

The second measure looked to defending the
city from an attack in the rear. At this time New
York City occupied only a very small section of
the southern part of the island which it has since

New York in 1776.   outgrown. A few farms and country
seats stretched up beyond Harlem, but
the major part of the island was to the city below
as the country to the town, retaining all its natural
features of hill and dale unimpaired. At this time,
too, the only exit from the island was by way of
King's Bridge,[4] twelve miles above the city, where

the great roads to Albany and New England turned off, the one to the north, the other to the east, making this passage fully as important in a military sense, as was the heavy drawbridge thrown across the moat of some ancient castle.

Fort Washington [5] was, therefore, built on a commanding height two and a half miles below King's Bridge, with outworks covering the approaches to the bridge, either by the country roads coming in from the north or from Harlem River at Fort Wash- the east. These works were never finished, but even if they had been they could not solve the problem of a successful defence, because it lay always in the power of the strongest army to cut off all communication with the country beyond — and that means the passing in of reën-forcements or supplies — by merely throwing itself across the roads just referred to. This done, the army in New York must either be shut up in the island, or come out and fight, provided the enemy had not already put it out of their power to do so by promptly seizing King's Bridge. And in that case there was no escape except by water, under fire of the enemy's ships of war.

One watchful eye, therefore, had to be kept constantly to the front, and another to the rear, between positions lying twelve to thirteen miles apart, and separated by a wide and deep river.

It thus appears that the defence of New York was a much more formidable task than had, at first, been supposed, and that an army of 40,000 men was none too large for the purpose, especially as it was wholly impracticable to reünforce King's Bridge from Brooklyn, or *vice versa*. But from one or another cause the army had fallen below 25,000 effectives by midsummer, counting also the militia, who formed a floating and most uncertain constituent of it. For the present, therefore, King's Bridge was held as an outpost, or until the enemy's plan of attack should be clearly developed; for whether Howe would first assail the works at Brooklyn, Bunker Hill fashion, or land his troops beyond King's Bridge, bringing them around by way of Long Island Sound, were questions most anxiously debated in the American camp.

However, the belief in a successful defence was much encouraged by the recent crushing defeat

that the British fleet had met with in attempting
to pass the American batteries at Charleston.
Thrice welcome after the disasters of the unlucky
Canada campaign, this success tended greatly to
stiffen the backbone of the army, in the face of
the steady and ominous accumulation of the British
land and naval forces in the lower bay. Then
again, the Declaration of Independence, read to
every brigade in the army (July 9), was received
with much enthusiasm. Now, for the first time
since hostilities began, officers and men knew
exactly what they were fighting for. There was
at least an end to suspense, a term to all talk of
compromise, and that was much.

Thus matters stood in the American camps,
when the British army that had been driven from
Boston, heavily reënforced from Europe, and by
The British calling in detachments from South Caro-
army. lina, Florida, and the West Indies, so
bringing the whole force in round numbers up to
30,000 men,[6] cast anchor in the lower bay.
Never before had such an armament been seen in
American waters. Backed by this imposing
display of force, royal commissioners had come

to tender the olive branch, as it were, on the point
of the bayonet. They were told, in effect, that
those who have committed no crime want no
pardon. Washington was next approached. As
the representative soldier of the new nation, he
refused to be addressed except by the title it had
conferred upon him. The etiquette of the contest
must be asserted in his person. Failing to find
any common ground, upon which negotiations
could proceed, resort was had to the bayonet
again.

---

[1] THESE were Poor's, Patterson's, Greaton's, and Bond's Massa-
chusetts regiments on April 21, two New Jersey, two Pennsylvania, and
two New Hampshire battalions on the 26th. See *Burgoyne's Invasion*
of this series for an account of the Canada campaign.

[2] THE numbers are estimated by General Heath (*Memoirs*, p. 51)
as high as 40,000. He, however, deducts 10,000 for the sick, present.
They were published long after any reason for exaggeration existed.

[3] THE Brooklyn lines ran from Wallabout Bay (Navy Yard) on the
left, to Gowanus Creek on the right, making a circuit of a mile and
a half. All are now in the heart of the city.

[4] KING'S BRIDGE was so named for William III., of England. It
crosses Spuyten Duyvil Creek. The bridge at Morrisania was not built
until 1796.

[5] FORT WASHINGTON stood at the present 183d street. Besides
defending the approaches from King's Bridge, it also obstructed the
passage of the enemy's ships up the Hudson, at its narrowest point
below the Highlands. At the same time Fort Lee, first called Fort

Constitution, was built on the brow of the lofty Palisades, opposite, and a number of pontoons filled with stones were sunk in the river between. The enemy's ships ran the blockade, however, with impunity.

6 THE British regiments serving with Howe were the Fourth, Fifth, Sixth, Tenth, Fourteenth, Fifteenth, Sixteenth, Seventeenth, Twenty-second, Twenty-third, Twenty-seventh, Twenty-eighth, Thirty-third, Thirty-fifth, Thirty-seventh, Thirty-eighth, Fortieth, Forty-second, Forty-third, Forty-fourth, Forty-fifth, Forty-sixth, Forty-ninth, Fifty-second, Fifty-fourth, Fifty-fifth, Fifty-seventh, Sixty-third, Sixty-fourth, and Seventy-first, or thirty battalions with an aggregate of 24,513 officers and men. To these should be added 8,000 Hessians hired for the war, bringing the army up to 32,500 soldiers. Twenty-five per cent. would be a liberal deduction for the sick, camp-guards, orderlies, etc. The navy was equally powerful in its way, though it did little service here. Large as it was, this army was virtually destroyed by continued attrition.

III

LONG ISLAND TAKEN

Up to August 22, the British army made no move from its camps at Staten Island. On their part, the Americans could only watch and wait. On this day, however, active operations began with British move the landing of Howe's troops, in great to L. Island. force, on the Long Island shore, opposite. This force immediately spread itself out through the neighboring villages from Gravesend, to Flatbush and Flatlands, driving the American skirmishers before them into a range of wooded hills,[1] which formed their outer line of defence. Howe had determined to attack in front, clearing the way as he went.

As the enemy would have to force his way across these hills, before he could reach the American intrenched lines around Brooklyn, all the roads leading over them were strongly guarded, except out at the extreme left, beyond Bedford village, where only a patrol was posted.[2] This fatal oversight, of which Howe was well informed,

Plan of   suggested the British plan of attack,
attack.   which was quickly matured and success-

fully carried out. It included a demonstration on the American left, to draw attention to that point, while another corps was turning the right, at its unguarded point.

A third column was held in readiness to move upon the American centre from Flatbush, just as soon as the other attacks were well in progress. When the flanking corps was in position, these demonstrations were to be turned into real attacks, which, if successful, would throw the Americans back upon the flanking column, which, in its turn, would cut off their retreat to their intrenchments.

This clever combination, showing a perfect knowledge of the ground, worked exactly as planned.

By making a night march, the turning column got quite around the American flank and rear unperceived, and on the morning of the 27th was in position, near Bedford, at an early hour,

waiting for the signal-guns to announce the beginning of the battle at the British left.

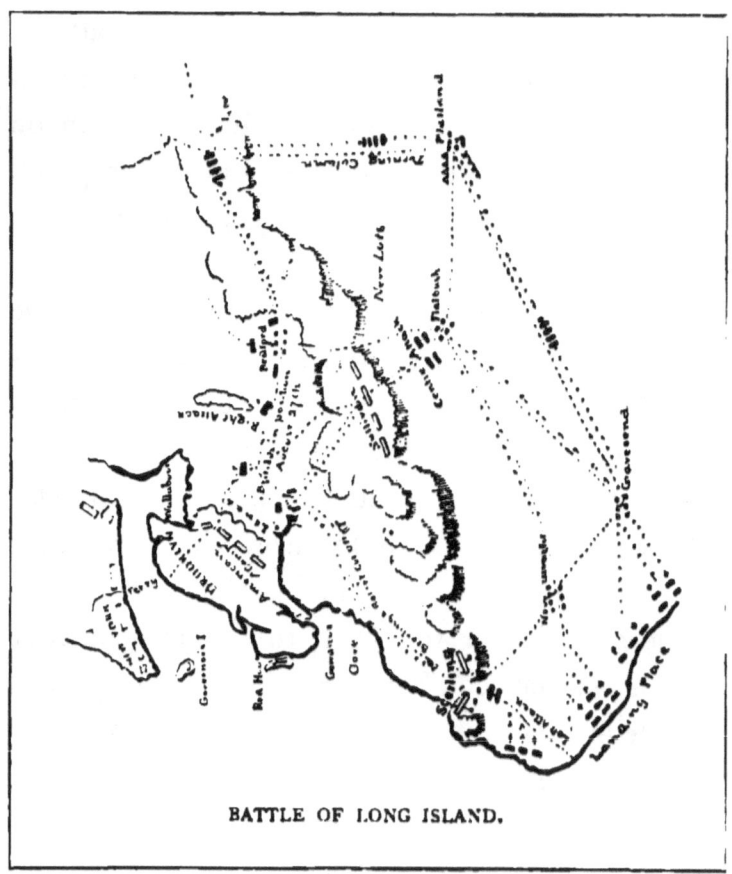

BATTLE OF LONG ISLAND.

Both columns then advanced to the attack.
Being strongly posted, and well commanded, the

Battle of Long Island. Americans made an obstinate resistance and did hold the enemy in check for some hours at one end of the line, only to find themselves cut off by the hurried retreat of all the troops posted at the passes on their left; for as soon as the firing there showed that the turning column had come up in their rear, these troops, with great difficulty, fought their way back to the Brooklyn lines, leaving three generals and upwards of 1,000 men in the enemy's hands.

The resistance met with by the enemy's turning corps may be guessed from what an officer[3] who took part has to say of it. "We have had," he goes on to relate, "what some call a battle, but if it deserves that name it was the pleasantest I ever heard of, as we had not received more than a dozen shots from the enemy, when they ran away with the utmost precipitation."

Though not in personal command when the action began, Washington crossed over to Brooklyn in time to see his broken and dispirited battalions come streaming back into their works. **Washington re-enforces.** Fearing the worst, he had called down two of his best regiments (Shee's and

Magaw's) from Harlem Heights, and Glover's
from the city, to reënforce the troops then engaged
on Long Island, but as has already been pointed
out, reënforcing in this manner was out of the
question. By making a rapid march, the Harlem
troops reached the ferry in the afternoon, after
firing had ceased. They were, however, ferried
across the next morning.

These movements would indicate a resolution to
hold the Brooklyn lines at all hazards, and were so
regarded, but during the two days subsequent to
the battle, while the enemy was closing in upon
28th and   him, Washington changed his mind,
29th.   preparations were quietly made to with-
draw the troops, while still keeping up a bold
front to the enemy, and on the night of the 29th
the army repassed the East River without accident
or molestation.

Having thus cleared Long Island, the British
extended themselves along the East River as far
as Newtown, that river thus dividing the hostile
camps throughout its whole extent. And though
New York now lay quite at his mercy, Howe
refrained from cannonading it, for the same reason

as Washington did from shelling Boston; namely, that of securing the city intact a little later.

In spite of this brilliant opening of the campaign, and outside of the noisy subalterns who were making their *début* in war, it was felt that the British army, fresh, numerous, and splendidly equipped, had acquitted itself most ingloriously in permitting the Americans to make their retreat from the island as they had, when the event of an assault must probably have been most disastrous to them.

On the other side defeat had seriously affected the *morale* of the Americans. Fifteen hundred men had been lost on Long Island. A great many more were now being lost through desertion. In Washington's own words the unruly militia left him by companies, half regiments or whole regiments, leaving the infection of their evil example to work its will among the well-disposed.

Losses so far.

Although the defence of New York had thus broken down at its vital point, a majority of generals favored still holding the city. To this end Washington now divided his forces, leaving 4,000 in the city, posting 6,500

New York to be held.

at Harlem Heights, and 12,000 at Fort Washington
and King's Bridge. Though furnished by a general
officer,[4] these figures really include the sick, who
were estimated at nearly 10,000, as well as the large
number detached on extra duty. Washington, himself, vaguely estimated his effective force at under
20,000 at this time.

As thus arranged, Harlem Heights, in the centre,
became the army headquarters for the time being,
Washington, by one of those little accidents that
sometimes arrest a passing thought, occupying the
house[5] of the same lady who had formerly refused
the offer of his hand in marriage, Miss Mary
Phillipse, later to accept that of Colonel Roger
Morris, his old companion in arms during Brad-
dock's fatal campaign.

---

[1] THIS range of hills includes the present Prospect Park and Green-
wood Cemetery.

[2] THIS weak point was the approach from the east where the Ja-
maica road crossed the hills into Bedford village. By striking this road
somewhat higher up, the enemy got to Bedford before the Americans,
guarding the hills beyond, had notice of their approach.

[3] CAPTAIN HARRIS, of the Fifth Foot.

[4] GENERAL GLOVER'S estimate.

[5] THE Morris House is still standing at 160th street, near 10th
avenue, N.Y., and is now occupied by Gen. Ferdinand P. Earle.

IV

NEW YORK EVACUATED

HOWE seems to have thought that so long as Washington remained in New York he might be bagged at leisure. In no other way can his dilatory proceedings be accounted for. Sixteen days passed without any demonstration on his part whatever. Meantime, however, the steady extension of his lines toward Hell Gate had operated such a change of opinion in the American camp that the decision to hold the city was now reconsidered, and the evacuation fixed for September 15. It was seen that the storm centre was now shifting over toward the American communications, but just where it would break forth was still a matter of conjecture.

Howe was fully informed of what was going on by his royalist friends in the city, and like the cat watching the wounded mouse while it is recovering its breath, he prepared to spring at the moment

his enfeebled adversary should show signs of returning animation.

All being ready, on the very day fixed for the
evacuation, Sir Henry Clinton crossed the East
River in boats from Newtown Bay to Kipp's Bay,
with 4,000 men, landed without opposition, owing
British seize to a disgraceful panic which seized
New York. the Americans posted there for just
such an emergency, and thus thrust himself in
between the Americans in the city and those at
Harlem Heights. Thus cut off, it was only at the
greatest risk of capture that the garrison below
was saved, with the loss of much artillery, tents,
baggage, and stores, by marching out on one road
while the enemy were marching in on another,[1]
as Clinton had immediately pushed on up the isl-
and, at the heels of the retreating Americans.

A captain of British grenadiers describes what
took place after the landing, in the following animated style:

" After landing in York Island we drove the
Americans into their works beyond the eighth
milestone from New York, and thus got possession
of the best half of the island. We took post

opposite to them, placed our pickets, borrowed a sheep, killed, cooked, and ate some of it, and then went to sleep on a gate, which we took the liberty of throwing off its hinges, covering our feet with an American tent, for which we should have cut poles and pitched had it not been so dark. Give me such living as we enjoy at present, such a hut and such company, and I would not care three farthings if we stayed all the winter, for though the mornings and evenings are cold, yet the sun is so hot as to oblige me to put up a blanket as a screen."

Each side now rested in possession of half the island, Washington of all above Harlem Heights, Howe of all below. His conquest was, however, near proving a barren one, at best, for within a week a third part of the city was laid in ashes, some say by incendiaries, some by accident.

Great fire, September 21.

The situation was now so far reversed that Washington seemed to be blockading Howe in the city.

Though it had little bearing upon the result of the campaign, one other event is deserving of brief mention here. Clinton's descent had been cleverly managed, out of Washington's sight. What were

the enemy proposing to do next? It was impera-
Captain Hale hanged. tive to know. To ascertain this Capt.
Nathan Hale volunteered to go over to
Long Island. At his returning he was arrested.
The papers found upon him betrayed his purpose
in going within the enemy's lines, and he was .
forthwith hanged in a manner that would have
disgraced Tyburn itself.

Howe's next move was probably conceived with
the twofold design, first of cooping Washington up
within the island, and second of capturing or
breaking up his entire army.

But again and again we are puzzled to account
for Howe's delays. Hard fighter that he unquestionably was, he seemed never in a hurry to begin.
There is even some ground for believing that in
Howe's delays. New York he had found his Capua. Be
that as it may, it is certainly true that
nearly a whole month passed by before the slug-
gard Sir William again drew sword.

Leaving Lord Percy to defend the lines below
Lands at Throg's Neck. Harlem with four brigades, at eight
o'clock P.M. of the 11th of October,
General Clinton with the reserves, light

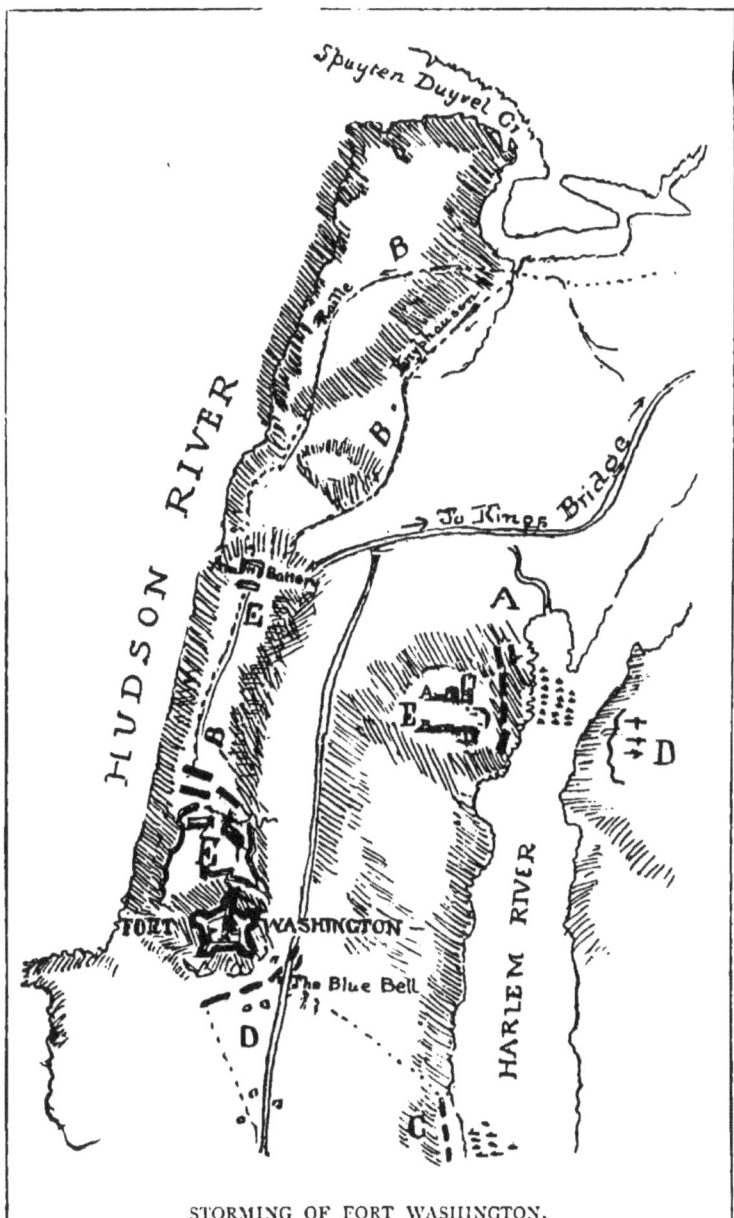

STORMING OF FORT WASHINGTON.

Explanation — E, American positions; A–C, British attacks by Harlem River; B, *via* King's Bridge; D, from Harlem Plains.

infantry and 1,500 Hessians, embarked on the East
River, passed through Hell Gate, and landed at
Throg's Neck,[2] in Westchester, early the next
morning.

Here he lay inactive for six whole days, within
six miles of the road on which Washington was
moving out from King's Bridge to White Plains;
for at the first notice given him of the enemy's
movements, which indeed had all along been
anxiously expected, Washington had been draw-
Washington ing out his forces from Harlem to
moves to King's Bridge, first sending forward
White Plains.
some light troops to delay Howe as
much as possible, until the army could get into
position. It is evident that but for Howe's delays
this purpose could not have been successfully
accomplished.[3]

Meantime the enemy had been bringing up reënforcements, and on the 18th, finding the mainland
too strongly held at Throg's Neck, for an advance
Howe from that point, they made another
marches to landing six miles beyond, whence they
give battle.
marched toward New Rochelle. From
here they again marched (22d) for White Plains,

where Washington was found (27th) drawn up in order of battle behind the Bronx, waiting for them.

Here Washington attempted to make a stand, but his right[4] being vigorously attacked and

Battle of White Plains, October 28. turned, he was forced to fall back upon a second position, in which he remained unmolested for several days, when (November 1) he moved still farther back, to the heights of North Castle, where he felt himself quite safe from attack.

Howe had now manœuvred Washington out of all his defences except Fort Washington, which by General Greene's advice was to be defended, though now cut off from all support.

Things remained in this situation until November 16, when the fort was assaulted on three sides, with the result that the whole garrison of about 3,000 men were made prisoners of war.[5] At some points the resistance was obstinate,

Fort Washington taken. notably at the north, and again at the east, where one of the attacking divisions attempted to gain the rocky shore back of the Morris House, under Harlem Heights. A British officer,[6] there present, says of it that

" before landing the fire of cannon and musketry
was so heavy that the sailors quitted their oars
and lay down in the bottom of the boats, and had
not the soldiers taken the oars and pulled on
shore we must have remained in this situation."

The loss of the garrison of Fort Washington,
2,000 of whom were regular troops, was univer-
sally regarded as the most severe blow that the
Effect on the American cause had yet sustained, and
army. it had a most depressing effect both
in and out of the army, but more particularly in
the army, as it tended to develop the growing
antagonism between the commander-in-chief and
General Lee, who had ineffectually advocated the
evacuation of Fort Washington when the army
Washington was withdrawn from the island. Lee's
and Lee. military insight had now been most
decisively vindicated. His antipathy to serving
as second in command became more and more
pronounced, and was more or less reflected by his
admirers, of whom he now had more than ever.
Worse still, it was destined soon to have the most
deplorable results to the army, the cause, and
even to Lee himself.

[1] A BRITISH brigade was sent down to the city in the course of the evening.

[2] A CONTRACTION of Throgmorton's Neck. As this was an island at high tide, the Americans quickly barred the passage to the mainland by breaking down the bridge.

[3] ON account of the want of wagons this was very slowly done, as the wagons had to be unloaded and sent back for what could not be brought along with the troops.

[4] THIS rested on Chatterton's Hill, some distance in front of the main line. Not having intrenched, the defenders were overpowered, though not until after making a sharp fight.

[5] AN excellent account of the operations at Fort Washington will be found in Graydon's *Memoirs*, p. 197 *et seq*.

[6] LIEUT. MARTIN HUNTER, of the Fifty-second Foot.

V

THE SITUATION REVIEWED

THE dilemma now confronting Washington was hydra-headed. Either way it was serious. On one side New England lay open to the enemy, on the other New Jersey. And an advance was also threatened from the North. If he stayed where he was, the enemy would overrun New Jersey at will. Should he move his army into New Jersey, Howe could easily cut off its communications with New England, the chief resource for men and munitions. Of course this was not to be thought of. On the other hand, the conquest of New Jersey, with Philadelphia as the ultimate prize, in all probability would be Howe's next object. At the present moment there was nothing to prevent his marching to Philadelphia, arms at ease. To think of fighting in the open field was sheer folly. And there was not one fortified position between the

The new situation.

Hudson and the Delaware where the enemy's triumphal march might be stayed.

Forced by these adverse circumstances to attempt much more than twice his present force would have encouraged the hope of doing successfully, Washington decided that he must place himself between the enemy and Philadelphia, and at the same time hold fast to his communications with New England and the upper Hudson. This could only be done by dividing his greatly weakened forces into two corps, one of which should attempt the difficult task of checking the enemy in the Jerseys, while the other held a strong position on the Hudson, until Howe's purposes should be more fully developed. With Washington it was no longer a choice of evils, but a stern obedience to imperative necessity.

Lee was now put in command of the corps left to watch Howe's movement east of the Hudson, The army loosely estimated at 5,000 men, and ordivided. dered back behind the Croton. Heath, with 2,000 men of his division, was ordered to Peekskill, to guard the passes of the Highlands, these two corps being thus posted within supporting distance. With the other corps of 4,000 men Washington crossed into New Jersey, going into **Washington in New Jersey.** camp in the neighborhood of Fort Lee, where Greene's small force was united with his own command.[1] Orders were also despatched to Ticonderoga, to forward at once all troops to the main army that could be spared. Fort Lee had thus become the last rallying-point for the troops under Washington's immediate command, and in that sense, also, a menace to the full and free control of the lower Hudson, which the guns of the fort in part commanded at its narrowest point. Howe determined to brush away this last obstruction without delay.

Regarding Fort Lee as no longer serving any important purpose, perhaps foreseeing that it would soon be attacked, Washington was getting ready to evacuate it, when on the night of November 19[2] Lord Cornwallis made a sudden dash across to the New Jersey side, passing Fort Lee unperceived, landed a little above the fort at a place **Fort Lee taken.** that had strangely been left unguarded, climbed the heights unmolested, and was only prevented from making prisoners of the whole garrison by its hurried retreat across the Hackensack. Everything in the fort, even to the kettles in which the men were cooking their breakfasts, was lost.

As regards any further attempt to stay the tide of defeat, all was now over. The enemy had obtained a secure foothold on the Jersey shore from which to march across the State, when and how he pleased. Unpalatable as the admission may be, the fact remains that the Americans had been everywhere out-generaled and out-fought. Nearly everything in the way of war material had been lost in the hurried evacuation of New York.[3] Confidence had been lost. Prestige had been lost. Clearly it was high time to turn over a new leaf. With this lame affair the first division of the disastrous campaign of 1776 properly closes, and the second properly begins. It had been watched with alternate hope, doubt, and despondency. Excuses are never wanting to bolster up failing reputations. The generals said they had no soldiers, the soldiers declared they had no generals; the people hung their heads and were silent.

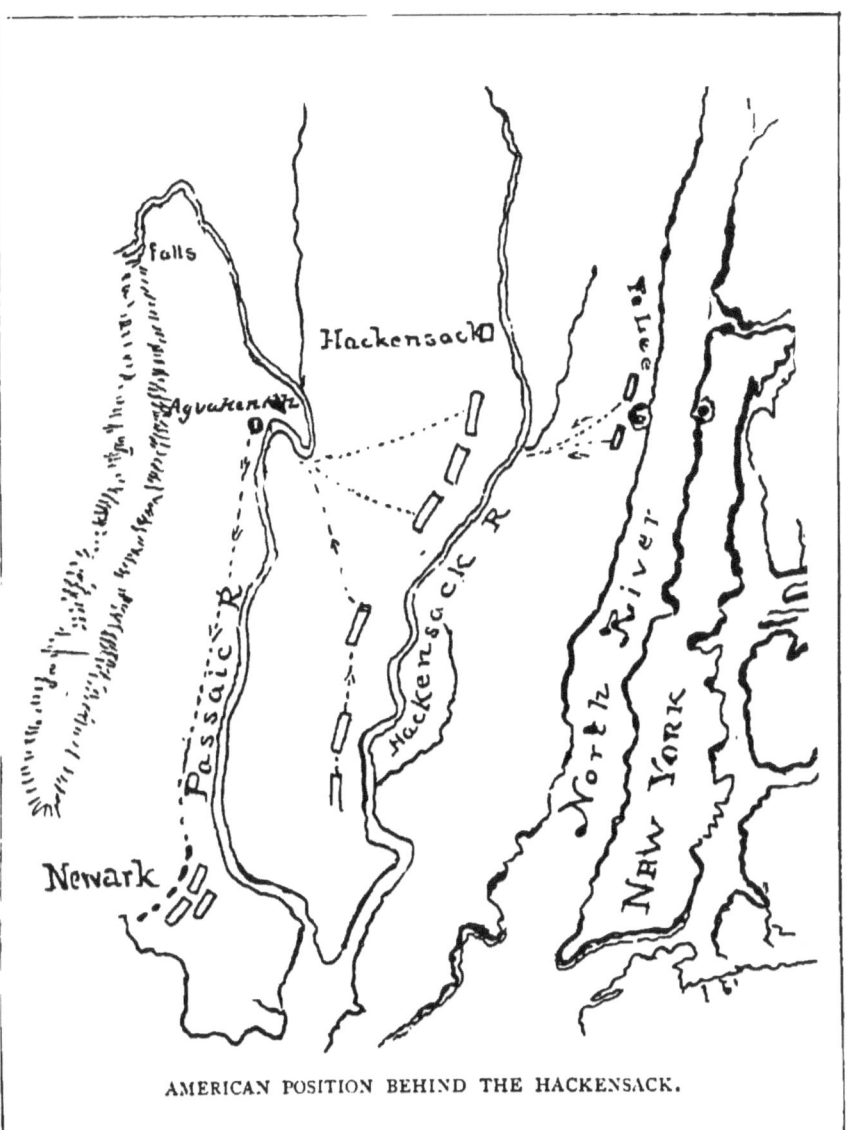

AMERICAN POSITION BEHIND THE HACKENSACK.

¹ THE Eastern troops remained on the east bank of the Hudson, under Lee's command, while those belonging to the Middle and Southern colonies crossed the Hudson with Washington. This disposition may have been brought about by the belief that the soldiers of each section would fight best on their own ground, but the fact is notorious that a most bitter animosity had grown up between them.

² THIS movement is assigned to the 18th by Gordon and those who have followed him. The 19th is the date given by Captain Harris, who was with the expedition.

³ AN enumeration of these losses will be found in Gordon's *American Revolution*, Vol. II., p. 360.

VI

THE RETREAT THROUGH THE JERSEYS

IT was now the 20th of November. In a few weeks more, at farthest, the season for active campaigning would be over. Thus far delay had been the only thing that the Americans had gained; but at what a cost! Yet Washington's last hopes were of necessity pinned to it, because the respite it promised was the only means of bringing another army into the field in season to renew the contest, if indeed it should be renewed at all.

Losses in battle, by sickness or desertion, or other causes, had brought his dismembered forces down to a total of 10,000 men, of whom 3,500 only were now under his immediate command, the Strength of the army. rest being with Lee and Heath. And the work of disintegration was steadily going on. Always hopeful so long as there was even a straw to cling to, Washington seems to have expected that

the people of New Jersey would have flown to
arms, upon hearing that the invader had actually
set foot upon the soil of their State.   Vain hope!
State of pub-   His appeal had fallen flat.   The great
lic feeling.   and rich State of Pennsylvania was
nearly, if not quite, as unresponsive.   Disguise it
as we may, the fire of '76 seemed all but extinct on
its very earliest altars, and in its stead only a few
sickly embers glowed here and there among its
ashes.   The futility of further resistance was being
openly discussed, and submission seemed only one
step farther off.   .

In one of his desponding moments Washington
turned to his old comrade, Mercer, with the question, "What think you, if we should retreat to the
back parts of Pennsylvania, would the Pennsyl-
vanians support us?"

Though himself a Pennsylvanian by adoption,
Mercer's answer was given with true soldierly
frankness.   "If the lower counties give up, the
back counties will do the same," was his dis-
couraging reply.

"We must then retire to Augusta County in
Virginia," said Washington, with grave decision,

" and if overpowered there, we must cross the Alleghanies."

A volume would fail to give half as good an idea of the critical condition of affairs as that brief dialogue.

First and foremost among the many causes of the army's disruption was its losses in prisoners. Not less than 5,000 men were at that moment dying by slow torture in the foul prisons or pestilential floating dungeons of New York. Turn from it as we may, there is no escaping the conviction that if not done with the actual sanction of Sir William Howe, these atrocities were at

Cruelties to prisoners. least committed with his guilty knowledge.[1] The calculated barbarities practised upon these poor prisoners, with no other purpose than to make them desert their cause, or if that failed, totally to unfit them for serving it more, are almost too shocking for belief. It was such acts as these that wrung from the indignant Napier the terrible admission that " the annals of civilized warfare furnish nothing more inhuman towards captives of war than the prison ships of England."

This method of disposing of prisoners was none the less potent that it was in some sort murder. Washington had not the prisoners to exchange for them, Howe would not liberate them on parole, and when exchanges were finally effected, the men thus released were too much enfeebled by disease ever to carry a musket again.

In brief, more of Washington's men were languishing in captivity in New York than he now had with him in the Jerseys. And he was not losing nearly so many by bullets as by starvation.

We have emphasized this dark feature of the contest solely for the purpose of showing its **Affects recruiting.** material influence upon it at this particular time. The knowledge of how they would be treated, should they fall into the enemy's hands, undoubtedly deterred many from enlisting. In a broader sense, it added a new and more aggravated complication to the general question as to how the war was to be carried on by the two belligerents, whether under the restraints of civilized warfare, or as a war to the knife.

Thrown back upon his own resources, Washing-

ton must now bitterly have repented leaving Lee
in an independent command. If there was any
secret foreboding on his part that Lee would play
him false, we do not discover it either in his orders
or his correspondence. If there was secret antipathy, Washington showed himself possessed of
almost superhuman patience and self-restraint,
for certainly if ever man's patience was tried
Washington's was by the shuffling conduct of his
lieutenant at this time; but if aversion there was
on Washington's part he resolutely put it away
from him in the interest of the common cause,
feeling, no doubt, that Lee was a good soldier
who might yet do good service, and caring little
himself as to whom the honor might fall, so the
true end was reached. It was a great mind lower-
ing itself to the level of a little one. But Lee
could only see in it a struggle for personal favor
and preferment.

After the evacuation of Fort Lee, Lee was urged,
unfortunately not ordered, to cross his force into
Retreat the Jerseys, and so bring it into coöp-
begins. eration with the troops already there.
The demonstrations then making in his front de-

cided Washington to fall back behind the Passaic,
which he did on the 22d, and on the same day
marched down that river to Newark. On the 24th
Cornwallis,[2] who now had assumed control of all
operations in the Jerseys, was reënforced with two
British brigades and a regiment of Highlanders.

Before this force Washington had no choice but
to give way in proportion as Cornwallis advanced,
until Lee should join him, when some chance of
checking the enemy might be improved. At
any rate, such a junction would undoubtedly have
made Cornwallis more circumspect. As Lee still
hung back, Washington saw this slender hope van-
ishing. He for a moment listened to the alternative
of marching to Morristown, where the troops from
the Northern army would sooner join him; but as
this plan would leave the direct road to Philadelphia open, it neither suited Washington's temper
nor his views, and he therefore adhered to his
former one of fighting in retreat. And though he
had failed to check Cornwallis at Newark he would
endeavor to do so at New Brunswick.

For New Brunswick, therefore, the remains of
the army marched, just as the enemy's rear-guard

was entering Newark in hot pursuit. On finding
himself so close to the Americans, Cornwallis
pushed on after them with his light troops, but as
Washington had broken down the bridge over the
Raritan after passing it, the British were brought
to a halt there.

Sustained by the vain hope of being reënforced
here, either by Lee or by new levies of militia
coming up as he fell back toward Philadelphia,
Washington meditated making a stand at New
Brunswick, which should at least show the exultant
enemy that there was still some life left in his
jaded battalions, and perhaps delay pursuit, which
was all that could be hoped for with his
**New
Brunswick** small force. Instead, however, of the
evacuated. expected reënforcement, the departure
of the New Jersey and Maryland brigades, still
so called by courtesy alone, since they were but
the shadows of what they had been, put this
purpose out of the question. Again Washington
reluctantly turned his back to his enemy.

Lee's troops were now the chief resource. What
few militia joined the army one day melted away
on the next. In Washington's opinion the crisis

had come. He therefore wrote to his laggard
lieutenant, " Hasten your march as much as possible or your arrival may be too late."

Fortunately Cornwallis had orders not to advance beyond New Brunswick. He therefore
halted there until he could receive new instructions, which caused a delay of six days
before the pursuit was renewed.[3]   On
the 7th Cornwallis moved on to Princeton, arriving there on the same day that Washington left
it.   This was getting dangerously near, with a
wide river to cross, at only one short march
beyond.

Deccem-
ber 7.

In view of the actual state of things, this retreat
must stand in history as a masterpiece of calculated temerity.   Keeping only one day's march
ahead of his enemy, Washington's rear-guard only
moved off when the enemy's van came in sight.
There is nowhere any hint of a disorderly retreat,
or any serious infraction of discipline, or any
deviation from the strict letter of obedience to
orders, such as usually follows in the wake of a
beaten and retreating army.   Washington simply
let himself be pushed along when he found resist-

ance altogether hopeless. In this firm hold on
his soldiers, at such an hour, we recognize the
leader.

[1] CAPTAIN GRAYDON (*Memoirs*) and Ethan Allen (*Narrative*), both
prisoners at this time, fix the responsibility where it belongs.

[2] CORNWALLIS (Lord Brome) was squint-eyed from effects of a blow
in the eye received while playing hockey at Eton. His playmate who
caused the accident was Shute Barrington, afterwards Bishop of Dur-
ham. He entered the army as an ensign in the Foot Guards. His
first commission is dated Dec. 8, 1756.

[3] THIS delay is chargeable to Howe, who kept the troops halted until
he could consult with Cornwallis in person as to future operations. The
question was, Should or should not the British army cross the Delaware?

VII

LEE'S MARCH AND CAPTURE

"HASTEN your march or your arrival may be too late. " When this urgent appeal was penned Lee had not yet seen fit to cross the Hudson, nor December 2 was it until Washington had reached and 3. Princeton that Lee's troops were at last put in motion toward the Delaware.

Hitherto Lee had been in some sort Washington's tutor, or at least military adviser, — a rôle for which, we are bound in common justice to say, Lee was not unfitted. But from the moment of separation he appears in the light of a rival and a critic, and not too friendly as either. In the beginning Washington had looked up to Lee. Lee now looked down upon Washington. Unquestionably the abler tactician of the two, Lee seemed to have looked forward to Washington's fall as certain, and to so have shaped his own course as to leave him master of the situation. In so doing he can-

not be acquitted of disloyalty to the cause he
served, if that course threatened to wreck the
cause itself.

It is only just to add that for troops taking the
field in the dead of winter, Lee's were hardly better
prepared than those they were going to assist.
General Heath, who saw them march off, says
that some of them were as good soldiers as any in
the service, but many were so destitute of shoes
that the blood left on the rugged, frozen ground,
in many places, marked the route they had taken;
and he adds that a considerable number, totally
unable to march, were left behind at Peekskill.
This brings us face to face with the extraordinary
and unlooked-for fact that instead of bending all
his energies toward effecting a junction with the

Lee's plans. commander-in-chief, east of the Delaware, in time to be of service, Lee had
decided to adopt an entirely different line of conduct, more in accord with his own ideas of how
the remainder of the campaign should be conducted. Meantime, as a cloak to his intentions,
he kept up a show of obeying the spirit, if not the
letter, of his instructions, leaving the impression,

however, that he would take the responsibility
of disregarding them if he saw fit. If he had
written to Washington, "You have had your
chance and failed; mine has now come," his words
and acts would have been in exact harmony.[1]

On the 7th Lee was at Pompton. This day an
express was sent off to him by Heath informing
him of the arrival of Greaton's, Bond's, and Porter's
battalions from Albany. Lee replied from Chatham
directing them to march to Morristown,
where his own troops were then halted.
December 7
and 8.
The prospect of this reënforcement, which in all
probability he had been expecting to intercept,
may account both for the slowness of Lee's march,
and for the closing sentence of his reply to Heath.
Here it is: "I am in hopes to reconquer (if I
may so express myself) the Jerseys. It was really
in the hands of the enemy before my arrival."

In halting as he did Lee was deliberately forcing a crisis with Washington, who was all this
time falling back upon his supplies, while the
British, having to drag theirs after them, could
only advance by spurts. Here was a rare opportunity for fighting in retreat being thrown away,

as Washington conceived, by Lee's dilatoriness in reënforcing him. Reluctant to abandon his last chance of giving the enemy a check, Washington seems to have thought of doing so at Princeton (ignorant that this spot was so soon to be the field of more brilliant operations) as a means of gaining time for the removal of his baggage across the Delaware. It was probably with no other purpose

Washington crosses the Delaware. that his advance, which had reached Trenton as early as the 3d, was marched back to Princeton, which Lord Sterling was still holding with the rear-guard as late as the 7th, when, as we have seen, Cornwallis made his forced march from Brunswick to Princeton, in such force as to put resistance out of the question.

December 8. Here he halted for seventeen hours, thus giving Washington time to reach Trenton, get his 2,200 or 2,400 men across the Delaware, and draw them up on the other side, out of harm's reach, just as his baffled pursuers arrived on the opposite bank.

Cornwallis immediately began a search for the means of crossing in his turn.[2] Here, again, he was baffled by Washington's foresight, as every

boat for seventy miles up and down the Delaware
had been removed beyond his adversary's reach.

On the day of this catastrophe, which seemed,
in the opinion not only of the victors, but of the
vanquished, to have given the finishing stroke to
the American Revolution, Lee's force, augmented
by the junction of the troops marching down to
join him, was the sole prop and stay of the cause
in the Jerseys.

That force lay quietly at Morristown until the
12th of the month, when it was again put in
motion toward Vealtown, now Bernardsville.

At this time a second detachment from the
army of the North, under Gates,[3] was on the
march across Sussex County to the Delaware.
Being cut off from communication with the com-
Gates   mander-in-chief, Gates sent forward a
arrives.   staff officer to learn the condition of
affairs, report his own speedy appearance, and
receive directions as to what route he should take.
Hearing that Lee was at Morristown, this officer
Lee taken.   pushed on in search of him, and at four
o'clock in the morning of the 13th, he found Lee
quartered in an out-of-the-way country tavern at

Baskingridge, three miles from his camp, and by just so much nearer the enemy, whose patrols, since Washington had been disposed of, were now scouring the roads in every direction. One of these detachments surprised the house Lee was in, and before noon the crestfallen general was being hurried off a prisoner to Brunswick by a squadron of British light-horse.

Lee's troops, now Sullivan's, with those of Gates, one or two marches in the rear, freed from the crafty hand that had been leading them astray, now pressed on for the Delaware, and thus that concert of action, for which Washington had all along labored in vain, was again restored between the fragments of his army, impotent when divided, but yet formidable as a whole.

Lee's written and spoken words, if indeed his acts did not speak even louder, leave no doubt as to his purpose in amusing Washington by a show of coming to his aid, when, in fact, he had no intention of doing so. He not only assumed the singular attitude, in a subordinate, of passing judgment upon the propriety or necessity of his orders, — orders given with full knowledge of the situation, — but proceeded to thwart them in a manner savoring of contempt. Lee was Washington's Bernadotte. Neither urging, remonstrance, nor entreaty could swerve him one iota from the course he had mapped out for himself. Conceiving that he held the key to the very unpromising situation in his own hands, he had determined to make the gambler's last throw, and had lost.

Although Lee's conduct toward Washington cannot be justified, it is more than probable that some such success as that which Stark afterwards achieved at Bennington, under conditions somewhat similar, though essentially different as to motives, might, and probably would, have justified Lee's conduct to the nation, and perhaps even have raised him to the position he coveted — of the head of the army, on the ruins of Washington's military reputation. Could he even have cut the enemy's line so as to throw it into confusion, his conduct might have escaped censure. With this end in view he designed holding a position on the enemy's flank,[4] arguing, perhaps, that Washington would be compelled to reënforce him rather than see him defeated, with the troops now

beyond the Delaware. Washington saw through
Lee's schemes, refused to be driven into doing
what his judgment did not approve, and the ten-
sion between the two generals was suddenly
snapped by the imprudence or worse of Lee
himself.

Captain Harris,[5] who saw Lee brought to
Brunswick a prisoner, has this to say of him:
" He was taken by a party of ours under Colonel
Harcourt, who surrounded the house in which
this arch-traitor was residing. Lee behaved as
cowardly in this transaction as he had dishonor-
ably in every other. After firing one or two
shots from the house, he came out and entreated
our troops to spare his life. Had he behaved
with proper spirit I should have pitied him. I
could hardly refrain from tears when I first saw ·
·him, and thought of the miserable fate in which
his obstinacy has involved him. He says he has
been mistaken in three things: first, that the
New England men would fight; second, that
America was unanimous; and third, that she
could afford two men for our one "[6]

[1] LEE had expected the first place and had been given the second. His successes while acting in a separate command (at Charleston) told heavily against Washington's reverses in this campaign; and his outspoken criticisms, frequently just, as the event proved, had produced their due impression on the minds of many, who believed Lee the better general of the two. Events had so shaped themselves, in consequence, as to raise up two parties in the army. And here was laid the foundation of all those personal jealousies which culminated in Lee's dismissal from the army. While his abilities won respect, his insufferable egotism made him disliked, and it is to be remarked of the divisions Lee's ambition was promoting, that the best officers stood firmly by the commander-in-chief.

[2] CORNWALLIS took no boats with him, as he might have done, from Brunswick. A small number would have answered his purpose.

[3] TICONDEROGA being out of danger for the present, Washington had ordered Gates down with all troops that could be spared.

[4] As WASHINGTON had been urged to do, instead of keeping between Cornwallis and Philadelphia.

[5] LORD GEORGE HARRIS, of the Fifth Foot.

[6] IT will be noticed that this account differs essentially from that of Wilkinson, who, though present at Lee's capture, hid himself until the light-horse had left with their prisoner.

VIII

THE OUTLOOK

To all intents the campaign of 1776 had now drawn its lengthened disasters to a close. It had indeed been protracted nearly to the point of ruin, with the one result, that Philadelphia was apparently safe for the present. But with Washington thrown back across the Delaware, Lee a prisoner, Congress fled to Baltimore, Canada lost, New York lost, the Jerseys overrun, the royal army stretched out from the Hudson to the Delaware and practically intact, while the patriot army, dwindled to a few thousands, was expected to disappear in a few short weeks, the situation had grown desperate indeed.

So hopeless indeed was the outlook everywhere that the ominous cry of " Every one for himself" — that last despairing cry of the vanquished — began to be echoed throughout the colonies. We have seen that even Washington himself seriously thought of retreating behind the Alleghanies, which was virtual surrender. Even he, if report be true, began to think of the halter, and Franklin's little witticism, on signing the Declaration, of, " Come, gentlemen, we must all hang together or we shall hang separately," was getting uncomfortably like inspired prophecy.

If we turn now to the people, we shall find the same apparent consenting to the inevitable, the same tendency of all intelligent discussion toward the one result. One instance only of this feeling may be cited here, as showing how the young men — always the least despondent portion of any community — received the news of the retreat through the Jerseys.

Elkanah Watson sets down the following at Plymouth, Mass.: "We looked upon the contest as near its close, and considered ourselves a vanquished people. The young men present determined to emigrate, and seek some spot where liberty dwelt, and where the arm of British tyranny could not reach us. Major Thomas (who had brought them the dispiriting news from the army) animated our desponding spirits

with the assurance that Washington was not
dismayed, but evinced the same serenity and
confidence as ever. Upon him rested all our
hopes."

At the British headquarters the contest, with
good reason, was felt to be practically over.
Unless all signs failed one short campaign would,
beyond all question, end it; for at no point were
the Americans able to show a respectable force.
In the North a fresh army, under General Burgoyne, was getting ready to break
through Ticonderoga and come down
the Hudson with a rush, carrying all before them,
as Cornwallis had done in the Jerseys. This
would cut the rebellion in two. On the same
day that Washington crossed the Delaware, Clinton had seized Newport, without firing a shot.
This would hold New England in check. In
short, should Howe's plans for the coming season
work, as there was every reason to expect, then
there would be little enough left of the Revolution
in its cradle and stronghold, with the troops at
New York, Albany, and Newport acting in well-
devised combination.

British
plans.

Brilliant only when roused by the presence of danger, Howe as easily fell into his habitual indolence when the danger had passed by. In effect, what had he to fear? Washington was beyond the Delaware, with the débris of the army he had lately commanded, which served him rather as an escort than a defence. If let alone, even this would shortly disappear.

Under these circumstances Howe felt that he could well afford to give himself and his troops a breathing-spell. This was now being put in train. Cornwallis was about to sail for England, on leave of absence. The garrison of New York disposed itself to pass the winter in idleness, and even those detachments doing outpost duty in the Jerseys, after having chased Washington until they were tired, turned their attention exclusively to the disaffected inhabitants. The field had already been reaped, and these troops were the gleaners.

To hold what had been gained a chain of posts was now stretched across the Jerseys from Perth Amboy to the Delaware, with Trenton, Bordentown, and Burlington as the outposts and New Brunswick as the dépôt, the first being well placed

either for making an advance, or for checking any
attempts by the Americans to recross the river.
Washington believed that the British would be in
Chain
of posts. Philadelphia just as soon as the ice was
strong enough to bear artillery.   If
the expected dissolution of his army had hap-
pened, no doubt the enemy's advanced troops
would have taken possession of the city at once.
And it is even quite probable that this contingency
was considered a foregone conclusion, since British
agents were now actively at work in Washington's
own camp, undermining the feeble authority which
everybody believed was tottering to its fall.

Be that as it may, the fact remains that active operations were for the present wholly sus-
pended.   At the officers' messes or in the barracks all the talk was of going home.   Besides,
if Howe had really wanted to take Philadelphia
there was nothing to prevent his doing so.   There
were no defences.   If saved at all, the city must
be defended in the field, not in the streets.

Bordentown being rather the most exposed,
Count Donop was left there with some 2,000
Hessians, and Colonel Rall at Trenton with 1,200

THE ATTACK ON TRENTON

to 1,300 more. Both were veterans. As these Hessians were about equally hated and feared, it was well reasoned that they would be all the more watchful against a surprise.

As soon as he had time to look about him, Donop at once extended his outposts down to Burlington, on the river, and to Black Horse, on the back-road leading south to Mt. Holly, thus establishing himself at the base point of a triangle from which his outposts could be speedily reënforced, either from Bordentown or each other. The post at Burlington was only eighteen miles from Philadelphia.

Rall and Donop.

In order to understand the efforts subsequently made to break through it this line should be carefully traced out on the map. In spots it was weak, yet the long gaps, like that between Princeton and Trenton, and between Princeton and Brunswick, were thought sufficiently secured by occasional patrols.

To meet these dispositions of the enemy Washington stretched out the remnant of his force along the opposite bank of the Delaware, from above Trenton to below Bordentown, looking chiefly to the usual crossing places, which were being vigilantly watched.

Under date of December 16 a British officer writes home as follows : " Winter quarters are now

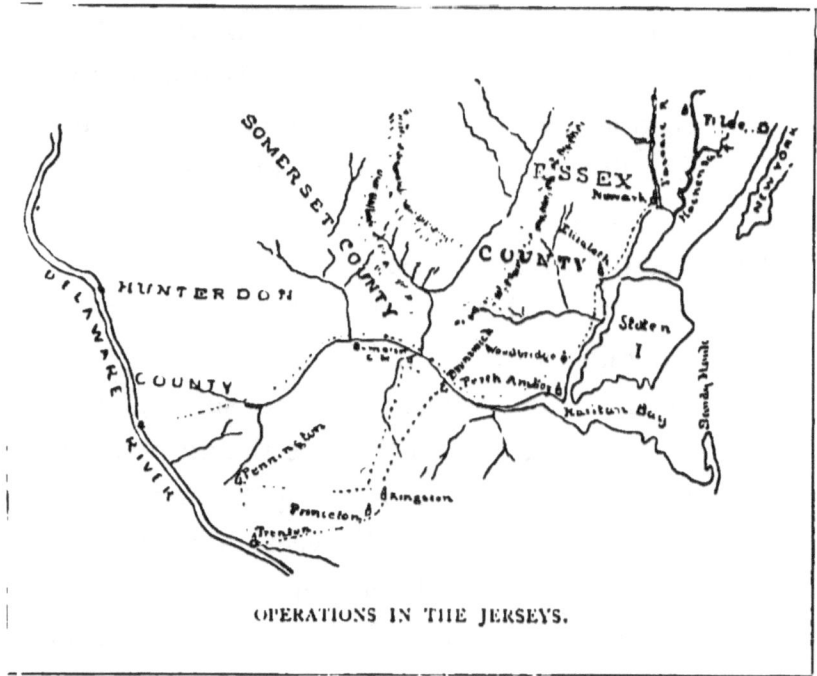

OPERATIONS IN THE JERSEYS.

fixed. Our army forms a chain of about ninety miles in length from Fort Lee, where our baggage crossed, to Trenton on the Delaware, which river, I believe, we shall not cross till next campaign, as

General Howe is returning to New York. I understand we are to winter at a small village near the
Raritan River, and are to form a sort of advanced
picket. There is mountainous ground very near
this post where the rebels are still in arms, and are
expected to be troublesome during the winter."

He then goes on to speak of the deplorable
condition in which the inhabitants had been left
by the rival armies, dividing the blame with im-
partial hand, and moralizing a little, as follows:
" A civil war is a dreadful thing; what with
the devastation of the rebels, and that of the
English and Hessian troops, every part of the
country where the scene of the action
has been looks deplorable. Furniture

Cruelties of
troops.

is broken to pieces, good houses deserted and
almost destroyed, others burnt; cattle, horses, and
poultry carried off; and the old plundered of their
all. The rebels everywhere left their sick behind, and most of them have died for want of
care."

This telling piece of testimony is introduced here
not only because it comes from an eye-witness, but
from an enemy. Beneath the uniform the man

speaks out. But his omissions are still more elo-
quent. It was not so much the loss of property,
bad as that was, as the nameless atrocities everywhere perpetrated by the royal troops upon the
young, the helpless, and the innocent, that makes
the tale too revolting to be told. In truth, all that
part of the Jerseys held by the enemy had been
given up to indiscriminate rapine and plunder. It
was in vain that the victims pleaded the king's protection. As vainly did they appeal to the human-
ity of the invaders. The brutal soldiery defied the
one and laughed at the other. Finding that the
promised pardon and mercy were synonymous with
murder, arson, and rapine, such a revulsion of feeling had taken place that the authors of these cruelties were literally sleeping on a volcano; and where
patriotism had so lately been invoked in vain,
hope of revenge was now turning every man,
woman, and child into either an open or a secret
foe to the despoilers of their homes. One little
breath only was wanting to fan the revolt to a
flame; one little spark to fire the train. All eyes,
therefore, were instinctively turned to the banks of
the Delaware.

IX

THE MARCH TO TRENTON

ENOUGH has been said to show that only heroic measures could now save the American cause. Fortunately Washington was surrounded by a little knot of officers of approved fidelity, whose spirit Spirit of the no reverses could subdue. And though officers. a calm retrospect of so many disasters, with all the jealousies, the defections, and the terror which had followed in their wake, might well have carried discouragement to the stoutest hearts, this little band of heroes now closed up around their careworn chief, and like the ever-famous Guard at Waterloo, were fully resolved to die rather than surrender. This was much. It was still more when Washington found his officers inspired by the same hope of striking the enemy unawares Post at which he himself had all along secretly Bristol. entertained. The hope was still further encouraged by a reënforcement of Pennsylvania

militia, whose pride had been aroused at seeing
the invader's vedettes in sight of their capital.
These were posted at Bristol, under Cadwalader,[1]
as a check to Count Donop, while what was left of
the old army was guarding the crossings above, as
a check to Rall.

To do something, and to do it quickly, were
equally imperative, because the term of the regular
troops would expire in a few days more, and no
one realized better than the commander-in-chief
that the militia could not long be held together
inactive in camp.

The isolated situation of Rall and Donop seemed
to invite attack. Their fancied security seemed
also to presage success. An inexorable necessity
called loudly for action before conditions so favor-
able should be changed by the freezing up of the
Rall's   Delaware when, if the enemy had any
danger.   enterprise whatever, the river would no
longer prevent, but assist, his marching into Philadelphia, and perhaps dictating a peace from the
halls of Congress.

Donop being considerably nearer Philadelphia
than Rall, was, as we have seen, being closely

watched by Cadwalader, whose force being largely drawn from the city had the best reasons for wishing to be rid of so troublesome a neighbor.

More especially in view of possible contingencies, which he could not be on the ground to direct, Washington sent his able adjutant-general, Reed,[2] down to aid Cadwalader. This action, too, removed a difficulty which had arisen out of Gates'

Gates sulking.

excusing himself from taking this command on the plea of ill-health.

Below Cadwalader, again, Putnam was in command at Philadelphia, with a fluctuating force of local militia, only sufficiently numerous to furnish guards for the public property, protect the friends,

In Philadelphia.

and watch the enemies, of the cause, between whom the city was thought to be about equally divided. Most reluctantly the conclusion had been reached that the appearance of the British in force, on the opposite bank of the Delaware, would be the signal for a revolt. Here, then, was another rock of danger, upon which the losing cause was now steadily drifting, — another warning not to delay action.

It was then that Washington resolved on mak-

ing one of those sudden movements so discon-
certing to a self-confident enemy. It had been
some time maturing, but could not be sooner put
in execution on account of the wretched condition
of Sullivan's (lately Lee's) troops, who had come
off their long march, as Washington expresses it,
in want of everything.

Putnam was the first to beard the lion by throwing part of his force across the Delaware.[3] Whether

A first move.   this was done to mask any purposed
movement from above, or not, it certainly
had that result. After crossing into the Jerseys
Griffin marched straight to Mt. Holly, where he
was halted on the 22d, waiting for the reënforcements he had asked for from Cadwalader. Donop
having promptly accepted the challenge, marched
against Griffin, who, having effected his purpose
of drawing Donop's attention to himself, fell back
beyond striking distance.

It was Washington's plan to throw Cadwalader's and Ewing's[4] forces in between Donop and
Rall, while Griffin or Putnam was threatening
Donop from below; and he was striking Rall
from above. Had these blows fallen in quick

succession there is little room to doubt that a much greater measure of success would have resulted.

Orders for the intended movement were sent out from headquarters on the 23d. They ran to this effect:

Cadwalader at Bristol, Ewing at Trenton Ferry, and Washington himself at McKonkey's Ferry, were to cross the Delaware simultaneously on the night of the 25th and attack the enemy's posts in their front. Cadwalader and Ewing having spent the night in vain efforts to cross their commands, returned to their encampments. It only remains to follow the movements of the commander-in-chief, who was fortunately ignorant of these failures.

Rall the object.

Twenty-four hundred men, with eighteen cannon, were drawn up on the bank of the river at sunset. Tolstoi claims that the real problem of the science of war " is to ascertain and formulate the value of the spirit of the men, and their willingness and eagerness to fight." This little band was all on fire to be led against the enemy. No holiday march lay before them, yet every officer and man instinctively felt that the last hope of the Republic lay in the might of his own good right arm.

Did we need any further proof of the desperate nature of these undertakings, it is found in the matchless group of officers that now gathered round the commander-in-chief to stand or fall with him. With such chiefs and such soldiers the fight was sure to be conducted with skill and energy.

Greene, Sullivan, St. Clair, Sterling, Knox, Mercer, Stephen, Glover, Hand, Stark, Poor, and Patterson were there to lead these slender columns to victory. Among the subordinates who were treading this rugged pathway to renown were **Strong array of officers.** Hull, Monroe, Hamilton, and Wilkinson. Rank disappeared in the soldier. Major-generals commanded weak brigades, brigadiers, half battalions, colonels, broken companies. Some sudden inspiration must have nerved these men to face the dangers of that terrible night. History fails to show a more sublime devotion to an apparently lost cause.

Boats being held in readiness the troops began their memorable crossing. Its difficulties and dangers may be estimated by the failure of the

two coöperating corps to surmount them. Of this
The Dela- part of the work Glover[5] took charge.
ware crossed. Again his Marblehead men manned
the boats, as they had done at Long Island; and
though it was necessary to force a passage by
main strength through the floating ice, which the
strong current and high wind steadily drove
against them, the transfer from the friendly to the
hostile shore slowly went on in the thickening
darkness and gloom of the waiting hours.

Little by little the group on the eastern shore
began to grow larger as the hours wore on.
Washington was there wrapped in his cloak, and
in that inscrutable silence denoting the crisis of a
lifetime. Did his thoughts go back to that eventful hour when he was guiding a frail raft through
the surging ice of the Monongahela? Knox was
there animating the utterly cheerless scene by his
loud commands to the men in charge of his pre-
cious artillery, for which the shivering troops were
impatiently waiting. At three o'clock the last
gun was landed. The crossing had required three
hours more than had been allowed for it. Nearly
another hour was used up in forming the troops

for the march of nine´ miles to Trenton, which
could hardly be reached over such a wretched
road, and in such weather, in less than from three
to four hours more. To make matters worse, rain,
hail, and sleet began falling heavily, and freezing
as it fell.

To surround and surprise Trenton before daybreak was now out of the question. Nevertheless,
Washington decided to push on as rapidly as possible; and the troops having been formed in two
columns, were now put in motion toward the
enemy.

The march was horrible. A more severe winter's night had never been experienced even by
the oldest campaigners. To keep moving was the
only defence against freezing. Enveloped in
whirling snow-flakes, encompassed in blackest
darkness, the little column toiled steadily on
through sludge ankle-deep, those in the rear judg-
ing by the quantity of snow lodged on the hats
and coats of those in front, the load that they
themselves were carrying. Not a word, a jest, or
a snatch of song broke the silence of that fearful
march.

At a cross-road four and a half miles from
Trenton the word was passed along the line to
halt. Here the columns divided. With one
Greene filed off on a road bearing to the left,
which, after making a considerable circuit, struck
into Trenton more to the east. Washington rode
with this division. The other column kept the
road on which it had been marching. Sullivan
led this division with Stark in the van. At this
moment Sullivan was informed that the muskets
were too wet to be depended upon. He instantly
sent off an aid to Washington for further orders.
The aid came galloping back with the order to " go
on," delivered in a tone which he said he should
never forget. With grim determination Sullivan
again moved forward, and the word ran through
the ranks, " We have our bayonets left."

All this time Ewing was supposed to be near-
ing Trenton from the south. In that case the
town would be assaulted from three points at once,
and a retreat to Bordentown be cut off.

---

[1] JOHN CADWALADER, of Philadelphia. His services in this campaign were both timely and important.

[2] JOSEPH REED succeeded Gates as adjutant-general after Gates was
promoted. Reed's early life had been passed in New Jersey, though

he had moved to Philadelphia before the war broke out. His knowledge of the country which became the seat of war was invaluable to Washington.

³ THIS force was under command of Colonel Griffin, Putnam's adjutant-general.

⁴ JAMES EWING, brigadier-general of Pennsylvania militia, posted opposite to Bordentown. In some accounts he is called Irvine, Erwing, etc.

⁵ COL. JOHN GLOVER commanded one of the best disciplined regiments in Washington's army.

X

TRENTON

VERY early in the evening there had been firing at Rall's outposts, but the careless enemy hardly gave it his attention. Some lost detachment had probably fired on the pickets out of mere bravado. The night had been spent in carousal, and the storm had quieted Rall's mind as regards any danger of an attack.[1]

But in the gray dawn of that dark December morning the two assaulting columns, emerging like phantoms from the midst of the storm, were rapidly approaching the Hessian pickets. All was quiet. The newly fallen snow deadened the rumble of the artillery. The pickets were enjoying the warmth of the houses in which they had taken post, half a mile out of town, when the alarm was raised that the enemy were upon

The attack.

them. They turned out only to be swept away before the eager rush of the Ameri-

cans, who came pouring on after them into the
town, as it seemed in all directions, shouting and
firing at the flying enemy. That long night of
exposure, of suspense, the fatigue of that ·rapid
march, were forgotten in the rattle of musketry and
the din of battle.

Roused by the uproar the bewildered Hessians
ran out of their barracks and attempted to form
in the streets. The hurry, fright, and confusion
were said to be like to that with which the imagina-
tion conjures up the sounding of the last trump.[2]

Street com-   Grape and canister cleared the streets
bats.   in the twinkling of an eye. The houses
were then resorted to for shelter. From these the
musketry soon dislodged the fugitives. Turned
again into the streets the Hessians were driven
headlong through the town into an open plain
beyond it. Here they were formed in an instant,
and Rall, brave enough in the smoke and flame
of combat, even thought of forcing his way back
into the town.

But Washington was again thundering away in
their front with his cannon. In person he directed
their fire like a simple lieutenant of artillery. Off

at the right the roll of Sullivan's musketry an-
nounced his steady advance toward the
Sullivan in action. bridge leading to Bordentown. The
road to Princeton was held by a regiment of rifle-
men. Those troops, whom Sullivan had been
driving before him, saved themselves by a rapid
flight across the Assanpink. Why was not Ewing
there to stop them! Sullivan promptly seized the
bridge in time to intercept a disorderly mass of
Hessian infantry, who had broken away from the
main body in a panic, hoping to make their escape
that way.

Not knowing which way to turn next, Rall held
his ground, like a wounded boar brought to bay,
until a bullet struck him to the ground with a
mortal wound. Finding themselves
Hessians surrender. hemmed in on all sides, and seeing the
American cannoneers getting ready to fire with
canister, at short range, the Hessian colors were
lowered in token of surrender.

A thousand prisoners, six cannon, with small-
arms and ammunition in proportion, were the
trophies of this brilliant victory. The work had
been well done. From highest to lowest the

immortal twenty-four hundred had behaved like
men determined to be free.

Now, while in the fresh glow of triumph, Washington learned that neither Ewing nor Cadwalader
had crossed to his assistance. He stood alone on
the hostile shore, within striking distance of the
enemy at Bordentown, and at Princeton. Donop,
The river   reënforced by the fugitives from Tren-
recrossed.   ton, outnumbered him three to two.
Reënforced by the garrison at Princeton, the
odds would be as two to one. All these enemies
he would soon have on his hands, with no cer-
tainty of any increase of his own force.

His combinations had failed, and he must have
time to look about him before forming new ones.
There was no help for it. He must again put the
Delaware behind him before being driven into it.

Washington heard these tidings as things which
the incompetence or jealousies of his generals had
long habituated him to hear. Orders were therefore given to repass the river without delay or
confusion, and, after gathering up their prisoners
and their trophies, the victors retraced their pain-
ful march to their old encampment, where they

arrived the same evening, worn out with their twenty-four hours' incessant marching and fighting, but with confidence in themselves and their leaders fully restored.

This little battle marked an epoch in the history of the war. It was now the Americans who attacked. Trenton had taught them the lesson that, man for man, they had nothing to fear from their vaunted adversaries; and that lesson, learned at the point of the bayonet, is the only one that can ever make men soldiers. The enemy could well afford to lose a town, but this rise of a new spirit was quite a different thing. Therefore, though a little battle, Trenton was a great fact, nowhere more fully confessed than in the British camp, where it was now gloomily spoken of as the tragedy of Trenton.

[1] HARRIS says that Rall had intelligence of the intended attack, and kept his men under arms the whole night. Long after daybreak, a most violent snow-storm coming on, he thought he might safely permit his men to lie down, and in this state they were surprised by the enemy. — *Life*, p. 64.

[2] GENERAL KNOX'S account is here followed. — *Memoir*, p. 38.

XI

THE FLANK MARCH TO PRINCETON

THE events of the next two days, apart from Washington's own movements, are a real comedy of errors. The firing at Trenton had been distinctly heard at Cadwalader's camp and its reason guessed. Later, rumors of the result threw the camps into the wildest excitement. Bitterly now these men regretted that they had not pushed on to the aid of their comrades. Supposing Washington still to be at Trenton, Cadwalader made a second attempt to cross to his assistance at Bristol on the 27th, when, in fact, Washington was then back in Pennsylvania.[1]

Cadwalader — crosses.

Cadwalader thus put himself into precisely the same situation from which Washington had just hastened to extricate himself. But neither · had foreseen the panic which had seized the enemy on hearing of the surprise of Trenton.

On getting over the river, Cadwalader learned

the true state of things, which placed him in a
very awkward dilemma as to what he should do
next. As his troops were eager to emulate the
brilliant successes of their comrades, he decided,
however, to go in search of Donop. He therefore marched up to Burlington the same afternoon.
The enemy had left it the day before. He then
made a night march to Bordentown, which was
also found deserted in haste. Crosswicks, another
outpost lying toward Princeton, was next seized by

At Borden-
town.
a detachment. That, too, had been
hurriedly abandoned. Cadwalader
could find nobody to attack or to attack him. The
stupefied people only knew that their villages had
been suddenly evacuated. In short, the enemy's
whole line had been swept away like dead leaves
before an autumnal gale, under that one telling
blow at Trenton.

Even Washington himself seems not to have
realized the full extent of his success until these
astonishing reports came in in quick succession.
As the elated Americans marched on they saw the
inhabitants everywhere pulling down the red rags
which had been nailed to their doors, as badges of

loyalty. " Jersey will be the most whiggish colony on the continent," writes an officer of this corps of Cadwalader's. "The very Quakers declare for taking up arms."[2]

In view of the facts here stated, Washington was strongly urged to secure his hold on West Jersey before the enemy should have time to recover from their panic. The temper of the people seemed to justify the attempt, even with the meagre force at his command. On the 29th he there-

Trenton re-occupied.

fore reoccupied Trenton in force. At the same time orders were sent off to McDougall at Morristown, and Heath in the Highlands, to show themselves to the enemy, as if some concerted movement was in progress all along the line.[3]

Meantime the alarm brought about by Donop's [4] falling back on Princeton caused the commanding officer there to call urgently for reënforcements. None were sent, however, for some days, when the

Princeton reënforced.

grenadiers and second battalion of guards marched in from New Brunswick. In evidence of the wholesome terror inspired by Washington's daring movements comes the account of the reception of this reënforcement by an eye-witness, Captain Harris, of the grenadiers, who writes of it: "You would have felt too much to be able to express your feelings 'on seeing with what a warmth of friendship our children, as we call the light-infantry, welcomed us, one and all crying, ' Let them come! Lead us to them, we are sure of being supported.' It gave me a pleasure too fine to attempt expressing."

Howe was now pushing forward all his available troops toward Princeton. Cornwallis hastened back to that place with the *élite* of the army. While these heavy columns were gathering like a storm-cloud in his front Washington and his generals were haranguing their men, entreating them to stay even for a few weeks longer. Such were the shifts to which the commander-in-chief found himself reduced when in actual presence of this overwhelming force of the enemy.

Through the efforts of their officers most of the New England troops reënlisted for six weeks — Stark's regiment almost to a man.[5] And these battalions constituted the real backbone of subsequent operations. Hearing that the enemy was at least ready to move forward, Cadwalader's and

Mifflin's troops were called in to Trenton, and
Washington concentrates preparations made to receive the attack
unflinchingly.   This force being all
assembled on the 1st of January, 1777, Washington posted it on the east side of the Assanpink,
behind the bridge over which Rall's soldiers had
made good their retreat on the day of the surprise, with some thirty guns planted in his front to
defend the crossing.   Washington and Rall had
thus suddenly changed places.

The American position was strong except on the
right.   It being higher ground the artillery commanded the town, the Assanpink was not fordable
in front, the bridge was narrow, and the left secured
His position, Jan. 2, 1777. by the Delaware.   The weak spot, the
right, rested in a wood which was
strongly held, and capable of a good defence ; but
inasmuch as the Assanpink could be forded two
or three miles higher up, a movement to the right
and rear of the position was greatly to be feared.
If successful it would necessarily cut off all retreat,
as the Delaware was now impassable.

On the 2d the enemy's advance came upon the
American pickets posted outside of Trenton,

driving them through the town much in the same manner as they had driven the Hessians. As soon as the enemy came within range, the American artillery drove them back under cover, firing being kept up until dark.

Having thus developed the American position, Cornwallis, astonished at Washington's temerity in taking it, felt sure of "bagging the fox," as he styled it, in the morning.

The night came. The soldiers slept, but Washington, alive to the danger, summoned his generals in council. All were agreed that a battle would be forced upon them with the dawn of day — all that the upper fords could not be defended. And if they were passed, the event of battle would be beyond all doubt disastrous. Cornwallis had only to hold Washington's attention in front while turning his flank. Should, then, the patriot army endeavor to extricate itself by falling back down the river? There seems to have been but one opinion as to the futility of the attempt, inasmuch as there was no stronger position to fall back upon. As a choice of evils, it was much better to remain where they were than be forced into

making a disorderly retreat while looking for
some other place to fight in.

Who, then, was responsible for putting the army
into a position where it could neither fight nor retreat? If neither of these things could be done
with any hope of success, there remained, in point
of fact, but one alternative, to which the abandon-
ment of the others as naturally led as converging
roads to a common centre. In all the history of
the war a more dangerous crisis is not to be met
with. It is, therefore, incredible that only one man
should have seen this avenue of escape, though
it may well be that even the boldest generals
hesitated to be the first to urge so desperate an
undertaking.

In effect, the very danger to which the little
army was exposed seems to have suggested to
Washington the way out of it. If the enemy
could turn his right, why could not he turn their
left? If they could cut off his retreat, why could
Washington's not he threaten their's? This was sub-
tactics.   limated audacity, with his little force;
but safety here was only to be plucked from the
nettle danger. It was then and there that Wash-

ington [6] proposed making a flank march to Princeton that very night, boldly throwing themselves
upon the enemy's communications, defeating such
reënforcements as might be found in the way, and
perhaps dealing such a blow as would, if successful,
baffle all the enemy's plans.

The very audacity of the proposal fell in with
the temper of the generals, who now saw the knot
cut as by a stroke of genius.   This would not be a
retreat, but an advance.   This could not be im-
puted to fear, but rather to daring.   The proposal
was instantly adopted, and the generals repaired
to their respective commands.

Replenishing the camp fires, and leaving the
sentinels at their posts, at one o'clock the army
filed off to the right in perfect silence
and order.   The baggage and some
spare artillery were sent off to Burlington, to still
further mystify the enemy.   By one of those sudden changes of weather, not uncommon even in
midwinter, the soft ground had become hard
frozen during the early part of the
night, so that rapid marching was
possible, and rapid marching was the only thing

Jan. 3, 1777.

March to
Princeton.

that could save the movement from failure, as
Cornwallis would have but twelve miles to march
to Washington's seventeen, to overtake them —
he by a good road, they by a new and half-worked
one. Miles, therefore, counted for much that night,
and though many of the men wore rags wrapped
about their feet, for want of shoes, and the shoe-
less artillery horses had to be dragged or pushed
along over the slippery places, to prevent their
falling, the column pushed on with unflagging
energy toward its goal.

Shortly after daybreak the British, at Trenton,
heard the dull booming of a distant cannonade.
Washington, escaped from their snares, was sounding the reveille at Princeton. The British camp
awoke and listened. Soon the rumor spread that
the American lines were deserted. Drums beat,
trumpets sounded, ranks were formed in as great
haste as if the enemy were actually in the camps,
instead of being at that moment a dozen miles
away. Cornwallis, who had gone to bed expecting to make short work of Washington in the
morning, saw himself fairly outgeneralled. His
rear-guard, his magazines, his baggage, were in

danger, his line of retreat cut off. There was

not a moment to lose. Exasperated
at the thought of what they would say
of him in England, he gave the order to press
the pursuit to the utmost. The troops took the
direct route by Maidenhead to Princeton; and
thus, for the second time, Trenton saw itself
freed from enemies, once routed, twice disgraced,
and thoroughly crestfallen and stripped of their
vaunted prestige.

Three British battalions lay at Princeton the
night before.[7] Two of them were on the march
to Trenton when Washington's troops were dis-
covered approaching on a back road. Astonished
at seeing troops coming up from that direction,

the leading battalion instantly turned
back to meet them. At the same time
Washington detached Mercer to seize the main
road, while he himself pushed on with the rest of
the troops. This movement brought on a spirited
combat between Mercer and the strong British
battalion, which had just faced about.[8] The fight
was short, sharp, and bloody. After a few vol-
leys, the British charged with the bayonet, broke

through Mercer's ranks, scattered his men, and even drove back Cadwalader's militia, who were coming up to their support.

Other troops now came up. Washington himself rode in among Mercer's disordered men, calling out to them to turn and face the enemy. It was one of those critical moments when everything must be risked. Like Napoleon pointing his guns at Montereau, the commander momentarily disappeared in the soldier; and excited by the combat raging around him, all the Virginian's native daring flashed out like lightning. Waving his uplifted sword, he pushed his horse into the fire as indifferent to danger as if he had really believed that the bullet which was to kill him was not yet cast.

Taking courage from his presence and example the broken troops re-formed their ranks. The firing grew brisker and brisker. Assailed with fresh spirit, the British, in their turn, gave way, leaving the ground strewed with their dead, in return for their brutal use of the bayonet among the wounded. Finding themselves in danger of being surrounded, that portion of this fighting British

regiment [9] which still held together retreated as
they could toward Maidenhead, after giving such
an example of disciplined against undisciplined
valor as won the admiration even of their foes.

While this fight was going on at one point, the
second British battalion was, in its turn, met and
routed by the American advance, under St. Clair.
This battalion then fled toward Brunswick, part of
the remaining battalion did the same thing, and part
threw themselves into the college building they
had used as quarters, where a few cannon shot
compelled them to surrender.

Three strong regiments had thus been broken
in detail and put to flight. Two had been prevented from joining Cornwallis. Besides the
killed and wounded they left two hundred and fifty
prisoners behind them. The American loss in
officers was, however, very severe. The brave
Mercer was mortally wounded, and that gallant
son of Delaware, Colonel Haslet, killed fighting
at his commander's side.

After a short halt Washington again pushed on
toward Brunswick, but tempting as the opportunity
of destroying the dépôt there seemed to him, it

had to be given up. His troops were too much exhausted, and Cornwallis was now thundering in his rear. When Kingston was reached the army therefore filed off to the left toward [10] Somerset Court House, leaving the enemy to continue his headlong march toward Brunswick, which was not reached until four o'clock in the morning, with troops completely broken down with the rapidity of their fruitless chase.

Washington could now say, " I am as near New York as they are to Philadelphia."

---

[1] CADWALADER seems to have done all in his power to cross his troops in the first place. His infantry mostly got over, but on finding it impossible to land the artillery — ice being jammed against the shores for two hundred yards — the infantry were ordered back. Indeed, his rear-guard could not get back until the next day. This was at Dunk's Ferry. The next and successful attempt took from nine in the morning till three in the afternoon, when 3,000 men crossed one mile above Bristol.

[2] Thomas Rodney's letter.

[3] HEATH was ordered to make a demonstration as far down as King's Bridge, in order to keep Howe from reënforcing the Jerseys. It proved a perfect flash-in-the-pan.

[4] PART of Donop's force fell back even as far as New Brunswick.

[6] STARK made a personal appeal with vigor and effect. His regiment had come down from Ticonderoga in time to be given the post of honor by Washington himself.

6 IN a letter to his wife Knox gives the credit of this suggestion to Washington, without qualification.

7 THESE were the Seventeenth, Fortieth, and Fifty-first.

8 THE hostile columns met on the slope of a hill just off the main road, near the buildings of a man named Clark, Mercer reaching the ground first.

9 THE Seventeenth regiment, Colonel Mawhood, carried off the honors of the day for the British.

10 THE position at Morristown had been critically examined by Lee's officers during their halt there. Washington had therefore decided to defend the Jerseys from that position.

XII

AFTER PRINCETON

IT had taken Cornwallis a whole week to drive Washington from Brunswick to Trenton; Washington had now made Cornwallis retrace his steps inside of twenty-four hours. In the retreat through the Jerseys there had been neither strategy nor tactics; nothing but a retreat, pure and simple. In the advance, strategy and tactics had placed the inferior force in the attitude menacing the superior, had saved Philadelphia, and were now in a fair way to recover the Jerseys without the expenditure even of another charge of powder.

While Washington was looking for a vantage ground from which to hold what had been gained, everything on the British line was going to the rear in confusion. Orders and counter orders were being given with a rapidity which invariably accompanies the first moments of a panic, and which tend rather to increase than diminish its effects.

What was passing at Brunswick has fortunately found a record in the diary of a British officer posted there when the news of Washington's coming fell like a bombshell in their camp. It is given word for word:

On the 3d we had repeated accounts that Washington had not only taken Princeton, but was in full march upon Brunswick. General Matthew (commanding at Brunswick) now determined to return to the Raritan landing-place, with everything valuable, to prevent the rebels from destroying the bridge there. We accordingly marched back to the bridge, one-half on one side, the remainder on the other, for its defence, never taking off our accoutrements that night.

On the 3d, Lord Cornwallis, hearing the fate of Princeton, returned to it with his whole force, but found the rebels had abandoned it, upon which he immediately marched back to Brunswick, arriving at break of day on the 4th. I then received orders to return to Sparkstown (Rahway?). Washington marched his army to Morristown and Springfield. At about the time I arrived at Sparkstown, a report was spread that the rebels had some designs upon Elizabethtown and Sparkstown. The whole regiment was jaded to death. Unpleasant this! Before day notice was brought to me by a patrol that he had heard some firing towards Elizabethtown, about seven miles off. I immediately jumped out of bed and directed my drums to beat to arms, as nothing else would have roused my men, they were so tired. Soon after this an express brought me positive orders to march immediately to Perth Amboy, with all my baggage. At between six and seven the rebels fired at some of my men that were quartered at two miles distance. I had before appointed a subaltern's guard for the protection of my baggage. This duty unluckily fell upon the lieutenant of my company, which left it without an officer, the ensign being sick at New York. I immediately directed my lieutenant, who was a volunteer on this occasion, to march with his guard, that was then formed, to the spot where the firing was, while I made all the haste I could to follow him with the battalion.

The lieutenant came up with them and fired upwards of twelve rounds, when, the rebels perceiving the battalion on the march, ran off as fast as they could. Had I pursued them I should perhaps have given a good account of them.

The company baggage-wagon was, however, carried off by the Americans, driver and all. The garrison got to Perth Amboy that night. Elizabethtown was evacuated at the same time. The narrative goes on to say:

The only posts we now possess in the Jerseys are Paulus Hook, Perth Amboy, Raritan Landing, and Brunswick.

Happy had it been if at first we had fixed on no other posts
in this province. . . . Washington's success in this
affair of the surprise of the Hessians has been the cause of
this unhappy change in our affairs. It has recruited the
rebel army and given them sufficient spirit to undertake a
winter campaign. Our misfortune has been that we have
held the enemy too cheap. We must remove the seat of
war from the Jerseys now on account of the scarcity of
forage and provisions.

The writer shows the wholesome impressions
his friends were under in this closing remark:
" The whole garrison is every morning under arms
at five o'clock to be ready for the scoundrels."

In New York great pains were taken to prevent
the truth about the victories at Trenton and
Princeton from getting abroad. False accounts
of them were printed in the newspapers, over
which a strict military censorship was established;
but in spite of every precaution enough leaked
out through secret channels to put new life and
hope in the hearts and minds of the long-suffering
prisoners of war.

It was one of the misfortunes of this most extraordinary campaign that every blow Washington
had struck left his army exhausted. After each

success it was necessary to recuperate. It was
now being reorganized in the shelter of its moun-
tain fastness, strengthened by a simultaneous
uprising of the people, who now took the redress
of their wrongs into their own hands. No forag-
ing party could show itself without being attacked ;
no supplies be had except at the point of the
sword. A host of the exasperated yeomanry
constantly hovered around the enemy's advanced
posts, which a feeling of pride alone induced him
to hold. Putnam was ordered up to Princeton,
Heath to King's Bridge, so that Howe was kept
looking all ways at once. Redoubts were thrown
up at New Brunswick, leading Wayne to remark
that the Americans had now thrown away the
spade and the British taken it up. Looking back
over the weary months of disaster the change on
the face of affairs seems almost too great for
belief. From the British point of view the campaign had ended in utter failure and disgrace. In
England, Edward Gibbon says that the Americans
had almost lost the name of rebels, and in America Sir William Howe found that he had to
contend with a man in every way his superior.

INDEX

AMERICAN Army, 12, 17 *note;* marches to N. York, 12; its efficiency, 14; weakened by detachments, 19, 24 *note;* reënforced, 19, 20; effectives in summer of 1776, 22, 24 *note;* defeated at L. Island, 29; losses there, 31; how posted after the battle, 31, 32; driven from N. York, 39; fights at White Plains and Fort Washington, 40; losses there, 41; is divided into two corps, 44; dissension in, 49 *note;* reduced numbers, 50; summary of losses, 52, 53; reaches the Delaware, 57; in position there, 75; is reënforced, 79; time expiring, 80; reënlistments, 97.

BEDFORD, L.I., seized by British, 27.

Bordentown, occupied by British troops, 71, 72; evacuated, 95.

British Army of subjugation, 23; by regiments, 25 *note;* takes the field, 27; drives the Americans from L. Island, 27 *et seq.;* in winter quarters, 72, 76.

Brooklyn Heights fortified, 20, 24 *note;* outer defences, 26; turned by British, 27, 28.

CADWALADER, Col. John, 80, 87 *note;* fails to get his troops across the Delaware, 83; succeeds better in a second attempt, 94; and occupies Bordentown, 95.

Clinton, Gen. Sir Henry, at N. York, 34; moves to Throg's Neck, 36; captures Newport, R.I., 70.

Cornwallis, Gen. Lord, surprises Fort Lee, 45; is reënforced, 55; pursues Washington, 55, 56, 57, 58 *note;* is unable to follow him beyond Trenton, 62, 67 *note;* has leave of absence, 71; hastens back to Trenton, 97; makes a forced march back to N. Brunswick, 106.

DECLARATION of Independence, read to the army, 23.

Donop, Col. Count, 72, 75; abandons Bordentown, 95.

EWING, Gen. James, 83, 87 *note.*

FORT Lee, 24 *note;* evacuated, 45, 49 *note.*

Fort Washington, built, 21, 24 *note;* assault and capture of, 40, 41, 42 *note.*

GATES, Gen. Horatio, brings troops from Ticonderoga, 63, 67 *note;* refuses a command, 81.

Glover, Gen. John, at L. Island, 30; at Trenton, 85, 88 *note.*

Greene, Gen. Nathaniel, advises the holding of Fort Washington, 40; at Fort Lee, 45; heads a column at Trenton, 87.

Griffin, Colonel, moves into the Jerseys, 82.

Trenton, occupied as a British outpost, 72; carried by assault, 89
et seq.; fruits of victory, 91; an
epoch in the war, 93; first abandoned, 93; then reoccupied, 96.

WASHINGTON, Gen., at N. York,
12; decides to act on the defen-
sive, 18 *note;* stands on his dig-
nity, 24; not in command at L.
Island, 29; orders its evacuation,
30; moves to White Plains, 39;
fights there, but has to fall back,
40; his dilemma, 43; decides to
divide his force, 44; crosses into
N. Jersey, 45; manœuvring for
delay, 50; rises above partisan-
ship, 54; directs Lee to join him,
54, 55; retreats to Newark, 55; to
New Brunswick, 56; troops leave
him, 56; at Princeton, 57; admirable retreat, 57; crosses the
Delaware, 62; determines on
striking the British outposts, 79,
80; his plan, 82, 83; marches on
Trenton, 83 *et seq.;* carries Trenton by assault, but is obliged to
recross the Delaware, 91, 92; but
reoccupies Trenton, 96; takes
post there, 98; steals a march on
Cornwallis, 101, 107 *note;* fights
at Princeton, 103; personal gal-
lantry, 104; marches to Somerset
C. H., 106.

White Plains, Washington concentrates at, 39, 42 *note;* action at, 40.

EVERY-DAY BUSINESS ·· NOTES ON ITS PRACTICAL DETAILS

Arranged for Young People by M. S. EMERY

Price, boards, 30 cents net. By mail, 35 cents.

AN accurate knowledge of how to attend to the every-day affairs of a business life is, indeed, a most valuable possession. The requirements of modern business life are manifold and exacting, demanding technical information, and, besides, quite a degree of what may justly be termed "cultivation." This valuable and indispensable book covers a wide range of information of much importance, and is designed as a text-book for schools, and for ready reference for young people and those who need such instruction as it contains. It treats in an attractive and clear manner subjects which bear on every-day callings, like "Letter-writing," by which so large a percentage of business is conducted; "Bills, Receipts, and Accounts;" "Post-Office Business," with instructions regarding late advantages and scope of accommodation; "Telegrams," "Express Business," "United States Money," "Savings Banks," "National Banks," "Bank Checks," "Notes and Drafts," "Mortgages," "Investment and Speculation," "Taxes," "Fire Insurance," and "Life Insurance." These are topics conveying a general idea of the worth of the book — topics about which business men must know, and covering that which they who would be business men must learn. Keeping relatively abreast of modern methods, the educators of our day see the necessity of imparting *business knowledge*, as well as that which is purely scientific, historical, or literary in its nature; hence, the adaptability of "Every-Day Business" to the necessities of American schools and our progressive ways of life.

MISS WEST'S CLASS IN GEOGRAPHY

By FRANCES C. SPARHAWK   Boards 30 cts   By mail 35 cts

"After making child-nature a special study, Miss Sparhawk offers this little book as its result. It is designed to be used as a supplementary reader for classes in geography, and in cases of very young children as preparatory to the definitions and statements of text-books, which to children so often mean nothing. Still, the author does not intend that because this book is used all verbal explanations should be done away with; and while it is designed to take the place of aimless and weary work, it is not at all intended to do away with work and substitute play in its stead The subjects treated preclude that idea. Such topics as the following require study and work on the part of both teacher and pupil: 'The Horizon,' 'Trees,' 'Vegetation,' 'Heat and Moisture,' 'Water-sheds,' 'Sun and Rain,' 'Highways and Barriers,' 'From the Lakes to the Gulf,' 'Cities,' 'Mountains and Rivers,' and many more important topics, including the continents." — *School Journal.*

'd by all booksellers and sent by mail postpaid on receipt of price

LEE AND SHEPARD Publishers Boston

TEACHERS' AIDS.

THE ELEMENTS OF PSYCHOLOGY
By GABRIEL COMPAYRÉ. Translated by William H. Payne, Ph.D., LL.D., Chancellor of the University of Nashville. Price, $1.00, net. By mail, $1.10.

METHODS OF INSTRUCTION AND ORGANIZATION IN THE GERMAN SCHOOLS
By JOHN T. PRINCE, Mass. State Board of Education. Cloth, $1.00, net Mailing price, $1.15.

METHODS AND AIDS IN GEOGRAPHY
For the use of Teachers and Normal Schools. By CHARLES F. KING, Master Dearborn School, Boston. Cloth. Illustrated. $1.20, net. By mail, $1.33.

REMINISCENCES OF FRIEDRICH FROEBEL
By BARONESS B. VON MARENHOLZ-BÜLOW. Translated by Mrs. Horace Mann. With a sketch of the life of Froebel by Emily Shirreff. Cloth, $1.50.

MOTHER-PLAY AND NURSERY SONGS
By FRIEDRICH FROEBEL. Translated from the German. Edited by Elizabeth P. Peabody. Quarto. Boards, $1.50, net. By mail, $1.75.

THE SPIRIT OF THE NEW EDUCATION
By LOUISA PARSONS HOPKINS, supervisor of Boston Public Schools. Clo. $1.50.

HOW SHALL MY CHILD BE TAUGHT?
Practical Pedagogy or the Science of Teaching. By Mrs. LOUISA PARSONS HOPKINS, supervisor in Boston Public Schools. Cloth, $1.00, net.

AN HOUR WITH DELSARTE
A Study of Expression. By ANNA MORGAN of the Chicago Conservatory. Illustrated with full-page figure illustrations. Quarto. Cloth, $2.00.

THE VOICE
How to Train It, How to Care for It. By E. B. WARMAN, A.M. With full-page illustrations by Marion Morgan Reynolds. Quarto. Cloth, $2.00.

GESTURES AND ATTITUDES
An Exposition of the Delsarte Theory of Expression. By EDW'D B. WARMAN, A.M., auther of "The Voice, How to Train It, How to Care for It," etc. With over 150 full-page illustrations by Marion Morgan Reynolds. Cloth, $3.00.

HANDBOOK OF SCHOOL GYMNASTICS OF THE SWEDISH SYSTEM
By BARON NILS POSSE. Cloth. Illustrated. Net, 50 cents. By mail, 55 cents.

THE SPECIAL KINESIOLOGY OF EDUCATIONAL GYMNASTICS. By BARON NILS POSSE. With Analytical Chart. Fully illustrated. Quarto. Cloth, 3.00.

FIRST STEPS WITH AMERICAN AND BRITISH AUTHORS
By ALBERT F. BLAISDELL, A.M. Illustrated. Cloth, 75 cents, net. By mail, 85 cents.

STUDY OF THE ENGLISH CLASSICS
A Practical Handbook for Teachers. By ALBERT F. BLAISDELL. Cloth, $1.00, net. By mail, $1.10.

THE ART OF PROJECTING
A Manual of Experimentations with the Port Lumiere and Magic Lantern. By Prof. A. E. DOLBEAR, M.E., Ph.D. New Edition, Revised. $2.00.

OBSERVATION LESSONS
For Teachers. By LOUISA PARSONS HOPKINS, Supervisor Boston Public Schools. Parts I., II., III., and IV. Paper, 15 cents, net, each part. Complete in one volume, cloth, 75 cents, net. By mail, 83 cents.

EDUCATIONAL PSYCHOLOGY
By LOUISA PARSONS HOPKINS, Supervisor Boston Public Schools. 50 cents.

HANDBOOK OF ENGLISH LITERATURE
In two volumes. By FRANCIS H. UNDERWOOD, A.M. American Authors. British Authors. Price, $2.00 per volume. By mail, $2 20.

LIFE AND WORKS OF HORACE MANN
Edited by GEORGE C. MANN. Five volumes. Cloth, $2.50, net, per volume.

Any of the above sent by mail on receipt of price.

LEE AND SHEPARD   Publishers   Boston.

TEACHER'S METHODS .'. .'. AND AIDS

THE SPECIAL KINESIOLOGY OF EDUCATIONAL GYM-NASTICS

By BARON NILS POSSE, M.G. Graduate Royal Gymnastic Central Institute, Stockholm, Sweden. Director Posse Gymnasium, Boston. With 267 illustrations and Analytical Chart, $3.00.

The previous editions of Baron Posse's Swedish System of Educational Gymnastics having been exhausted, and a new edition demanded, the author has taken the opportunity to completely revise and enlarge it, making it the most complete and practical treatise on Educational Gymnastics in the English language. Although the title is changed to " Special Kinesiology," the basis of the work is the Swedish system, which the author holds must be the foundation of all rational gymnastics, " since, to-day, it is the only system whose details have been elucidated by and derived from Mechanics, Anatomy, Physiology, and Psychology, and whose theories have survived the scrutiny of scientists all over the world." Many tables of exercises have been added, together with an analytical chart of the system, which will be of great value to all students and teachers. Size of chart, 18 x 22 inches.

THE VOICE

How to train it How to care for it By E. B. WARMAN A.M. With full-page illustrations by MARIAN MORGAN REYNOLDS Quarto cloth $2.00

" The book is intended for ministers, lecturers, readers, actors, singers, teachers, and public speakers, and the special conditions applicable to each class are pointed out in connection with the general subject. The use and abuse of the vocal organs is considered, and their legitimate functions emphasized as illustrated by their anatomy, hygiene, and physiology. The breathing and vocal exercises for the culture and development of the human voice are made clear by diagrams as well as descriptions, and the fruits of the author's long experience as a teacher are embodied in this eminently practical treatise." — *Critic.*

AN HOUR WITH DELSARTE

A Study of Expression by ANNA MORGAN of the Chicago Conservatory Illustrated by ROSA MUELLER SPRAGUE and MARIAN REYNOLDS with full-page figure illustrations 4to cloth $2.00

" This beautiful quarto volume presents the ideas of Delsarte in words which all may understand. It is explicit and comprehensible. No one can read this book or study its twenty-two graceful and graphic illustrations without perceiving the possibility of adding strength and expression to gestures and movements, as well as simplicity and ease. Mr. Turveydrop went through life with universal approval, simply by his admirable ' deportment.' Every young person may profitably take a hint from his success, and this book will be found invaluable as an instructor." — *Woman's Journal, Boston.*

Sold by all booksellers, and sent by mail, postpaid, on receipt of price.

LEE AND SHEPARD Publishers Boston

HISTORICAL HANDBOOKS

Reference Handbook of American History

By the LIBRARY METHOD For Secondary Schools Period of the Constitution 1789–1889 By A. W. BACHELER Principal of the High School Gloucester Mass. Interleaved Price 50 cents *net*

In this selection of topics for study and research, the important events of the History of the United States are emphasized, the relation of cause to effect is clearly presented. The success of the method has been so well established by experience that this attempt to bring the system within the reach of every student of United States history will be gratefully received.

The Study of English History

By the LABORATORY METHOD By MARY E. WILDER
Interleaved Price 40 cents *net*

This manual, which was prepared by the author for use in her class-room, has proven of such value that many educators have desired it for use in other schools.

The work embraces English History from Ancient England until the present time and is covered by a very full list of topics which are divided into periods. At the end of each period a list of historical novels and dramas is given. The work contains a full list of the authorities mentioned, together with several minor lists. Hints are also given for teachers unaccustomed to laboratory method.

The Study of Roman History

By the LABORATORY METHOD By CAROLINE E. TRASK
Interleaved Price 40 cents

Topics for the Study of Greek Mythology

BASED ON BULFINCH'S "AGE OF FABLE" By ANNA GOODING DODGE, former teacher of English Literature in Arlington High School Price 20 cents *net* By mail 22 cents

This is a set of topics prepared for a systematic study of Mythology. The introduction of a separate course on this subject for high-school pupils has proved most successful and valuable both to classical and English scholars. These topics will be found of invaluable service to teachers and students in this study.

The Study of Greek History

By the LABORATORY METHOD By CAROLINE E. TRASK

LEE AND SHEPARD Publishers Boston

STORIES AMERICAN ***
OF ***** HISTORY

Four Books. Cloth, Illustrated. Price for each book, 50 cents. Boards, 30 cents net. By mail, 35 cents

FIRST SERIES

STORIES OF AMERICAN HISTORY. By N. S. Dodge. As a reading-book for the younger classes in public and private schools (by many of which it has been adopted), it will be found of great value.

"Nobody knows better than the author how to make a good story out of even the driest matters of fact. . . . Here are twenty-two of such stories; and they are chosen with a degree of skill which of itself would indicate its author's fitness for the task, even if we had no other evidence of that fitness. There is no better, purer, more interesting, or more instructive book for boys." — *New York Hearth and Home.*

SECOND SERIES

NOBLE DEEDS OF OUR FATHERS. As told by Soldiers of the Revolution gathered around the Old Bell of Independence. Revised and adapted from Henry C. Watson.

"Every phase of the struggle is presented, and the moral and religious character of our forefathers, even when engaged in deadly conflict, is depicted with great clearness. The young reader — indeed, older readers will like the stories — will be deeply interested in the story of Lafayette's return to this country, of reminiscences of Washington, of the night before the battle of Brandywine, of the first prayer in Congress, of the patriotic women of that day, stories of adventure regarding Gen. Wayne, the traitor Arnold, the massacre of Wyoming, the capture of Gen. Prescott, and in other narratives equally interesting and important." — *Norwich Bulletin.*

THIRD SERIES

THE BOSTON TEA PARTY, and other Stories of the Revolution. Relating many Daring Deeds of the Old Heroes. By Henry C. Watson.

"The tales are full of interesting material, they are told in a very graphic manner, and give many incidents of personal daring and descriptions of famous men and places. General Putnam's escape, the fight at Concord, the patriotism of Mr. Borden, the battle of Bunker Hill, the battle of Oriskany, the mutiny at Morristown, and the exploits of Peter Francisco are among the subjects. Books such as this have a practical value and an undeniable charm. History will never be dull so long as it is represented with so much brightness and color." — *Philadelphia Record.*

STORIES OF THE CIVIL WAR. By Albert M. Blaisdell, A.M., author of "First Steps with American and British Authors," "Readings from the Waverley Novels," "Blaisdell's Physiologies," etc. Illustrated. Library Edition, Cloth, $1.00. School Edition, Boards, 30 cents, net; by mail, 35 cents.

"An exceedingly interesting collection of true stories of thrilling events and adventures of the brave men who fought during the Civil War. The author aims to present recitals of graphic interest and founded on fact; to preserve those written by eye-witnesses or participants in the scenes described; and especially to stimulate a greater love and reverence for our beloved land and its institutions, in the character of the selections presented.

LEE AND SHEPARD Publishers Boston

DECISIVE ·· ·· AMERICAN ·· EVENTS IN ·· HISTORY

THE BATTLE OF GETTYSBURG. — 1863

By SAMUEL ADAMS DRAKE, with explanatory notes and plans. Cloth, 50 cents.

Mr. Drake's work needs no introduction; he is known as a careful student and an interesting writer. In the present volume he has treated his subject with enthusiasm. In eleven chapters he sets before his readers a graphic description of that fearful carnage, beginning with a description of the country and an account of the invasion, and ending with the story of the retreat and the result of the battle. The book is carefully edited, with copious notes, and is evidently designed for use in schools as well as for private study. It contains, in addition, the list of officers of the Army of the Potomac at the time of the battle, and an accurate index of the book. — *Lowell Times.*

THE TAKING OF LOUISBURG — 1745

By SAMUEL ADAMS DRAKE, author of " Burgoyne's Invasion of 1777, etc. Cloth, illustrated, 50 cents.

Mr. Drake's "The Taking of Louisburg " well deserves a place in the series of " Decisive Events in American History :" for the celebrated fortress was once the key and stronghold of French power in Canada, and its unexpected capture by a seemingly inadequate force was the beginning of the inglorious war between the French and English in America. Mr. Drake gives the history in a simple and concise style that makes it attractive, and impresses its incidents upon the memory in vivid colors, the illustrations increasing the effect of the text. It is just the book to arouse in the minds of young readers a deep interest in American history.

BURGOYNE'S INVASION OF 1777

With an outline sketch of the American Invasion of Canada, 1775-76, by SAMUEL ADAMS DRAKE. Price 50 cents.

" The invasion of Burgoyne holds its place as one of the most important events of the Revolutionary struggle. The author is well fitted by his line of study and investigation to write such a book. Few men are more familiar with the localities than he, and few more successful in description of place and action. He not only writes veritable history, but he gives to the record a sort of dramatic interest and fervor. Those who are familiar with the story will be delighted to go over the ground again with so enthusiastic a companion as Mr. Drake· — *Troy Budget.*

THE CAMPAIGN OF TRENTON — 1776-77

By SAMUEL ADAMS DRAKE. Price, 50 cents.

Sold by all booksellers, and sent by mail, postpaid, on receipt of price

LEE AND SHEPARD Publishers Boston

www.ingramcontent.com/pod-product-compliance
Lightning Source LLC
Chambersburg PA
CBHW020756020726
47495CB00008B/2455